it will be Forever

a rock creek romance

by

Jennifer
Rodewald

WORDS THAT EDIFY
Rooted Publishing

Printed in the United States of America
First Printing, 2019

Cover Design by Jennifer Rodewald
Cover photos from www.Lightstock.com

Published by Rooted Publishing
McCook, NE 69001

Visit the author's website at: https://authorjenrodewald.com

Things I would tell twenty-year-old me:
Embrace the beauty of life.
Even if that means living
simply
quietly
humbly
Look for the extraordinary in unexpected places.
In the end, you're the only one who gets to live your life.

JENNIFER RODEWALD

Chapter One

"LOOK. I'M LITERALLY BEGGING YOU."

Andrea Rustin planted both knees on the area rug that thinly disguised the industrial linoleum tiles of her dorm room floor. "You have to come with me. You have to protect me."

Janelle snorted and rolled her eyes. "Drama much?"

"Come on. We're friends, right?" Dre gripped Janelle's arm with desperate strength.

"You really should be majoring in theater. If that ain't a fact, God's a 'possum."

"I'm not kidding with this. I need you. This is a best girlfriend emergency here, and I'm dialing your number."

"Let me get this straight." Janelle leaned back against the couch, her amusement vivid and a little bit of wicked in her grin. "You want me to travel thirteen hours north, toward winter and snow, to a place that will have not much to offer come Black Friday, and miss Thanksgiving with my twisted and wildly dysfunctional family so that I can eat turkey with yours?"

"My brother is dysfunctional. You won't have to miss out on that part." Dre plopped onto the cushion next to Janelle and crossed her arms. "And missing Black Friday is my gift to you. You know you'll overspend and then agonize over the guilt, and then you'll go on a type-A, budget-every-penny, shame-driven return binge Saturday morning, which will be miserable for you and annoying to everyone else. So really, I'm saving you, not to mention all of those you may come into contact with over the long weekend. Because I'm that kind of a best friend. You're welcome in advance."

Janelle raised an eyebrow. "What's his name?"

"What?"

"The yellowjacket in your outhouse."

Dre snorted an unfeminine laugh. Living with Janelle had been quite a cultural education. "What under high heaven does that mean?"

"The guy I'm supposed to be saving you from." Janelle leaned closer, eyes pinched. "I need a name here before I can even consider this."

Andrea sighed. It came out more like a growl. "Tommy."

"Tommy?" Janelle waited, judgment thick in her pause.

Though heat swirled up her chest and crept into her cheeks, Dre refused to add more fuel to Janelle's mocking. It sounded ridiculous, even in her own head. Sitting there begging Janelle to drive from Texas to Nebraska with her for their Thanksgiving break all because her brother, Paul, had called and casually mentioned that Tom Kent was going to hang around for the holiday.

Why? She'd spat the word into the phone like she'd had unsweetened cocoa on her tongue.

Paul had chuckled. His easy-there, my perfectionist little sister, don't get your panties in a bunch kind of laugh. She hated that laugh.

Tom's family is down in Kansas now, taking over his grandpa's farm. Said he wanted to stay in Rock Creek. I didn't dive into an inquisition about it. Not sure why you need to know.

Of course he wouldn't need to know why Tommy was staying. Tommy was and always had been Paul's cover. His enabler. His quiet, appears-to-be-perfect best buddy who could do no wrong except turn a blind eye to all the stupid crap Paul did that landed him at Boys Town. Except that one time. Not to mention—

She'd ended that dumb line of thinking, because really, she didn't care. Tommy could do whatever he wanted. It was his life. His veiled-from-Paul-but-not-from-her life.

Janelle didn't need to know all of that. So Dre kept her lips pinned shut.

"Tommy." Janelle shook her head. "You're putting me between you and a guy who still goes by Tommy?"

Dang. Why'd she go and use the name she'd used through her growing up? Made it sound like they were childhood friends. Or something.

They were. Childhood friends, that was. Sort of. Tommy and Paul had been everywhere but Boys Town together, and from what Mom had said, Tommy had gone to Omaha a few times too. To check up on his buddy, whom he'd helped land in the strict alternative program designed to help troubled youth find the straight and narrow. Paul had known where the straight and narrow was every bit as well as Tommy had. Just thought it was more interesting to stay off it. At least he wasn't a hypocrite about it. Tommy though? He kept up a good-boy appearance to most. His mom, her mom, her brother—they all thought he was something else.

"He's not as innocuous as he sounds," Dre muttered.

Yeah. He was something else, all right.

"You know that there reeks of dead skunk?" Grabbing a throw pillow and hugging it to her middle, Janelle leaned toward Dre. "Maybe a story?"

Dre put on her blank-front expression. "Not between Tom and me. Nope."

"But a story still." Janelle wore certainty with all the comfort and ease of a pair of sweats. "Is he cute?"

"Cute? No." Dre cocked her head. "Thick blond curls, steel-blue eyes, shy but ornery kind of smile. Try an entrée of *crazy good looking* with a heaping side of *knows it*."

"Ah. The kind who can strut sitting down. So…"

"So nothing. He's a player, Janelle. And you're resolute. Got enough life experience behind you to read *trouble* when it's spelled out in boldface caps on some guy's forehead. So I trust that you'll be in no danger with his charming smile, easy compliments, and ability to gaze into your eyes like you might have the heavens hidden deep within."

Eyebrows raised, Janelle's expression moved from certainty to all-out hilarity. "Very poetic. You're way too wrapped up in this. What on earth did he do to you?"

For the love.

An eye roll. A quick push to her feet. Dre locked down the insecurities that had messed with her heart and mind for way too long. She was *not* that girl. Not now. Not anymore. Moving away for college had been the best decision of her life. Almost four full years now. Away from Paul and all his crap. Away from the small town that seemed to lock her in like a pressure cooker with all of its expectations and disappointments. Here, she was able to breathe. To look deep inside of herself and figure some stuff out. Who she was. Who she wasn't.

And this she knew for sure. She wasn't needy or rebellious or demanding. Wasn't her brother. And she wasn't willing to go back to wondering who the heck she was in the middle of his enormous mess and everything it took for their family to deal with it.

No more pulling Paul out of drunken brawls. Praying that he wouldn't drown in his fermented vomit after she'd drifted off to sleep, or die due to alcohol poisoning, or rec drug overdose, or at the hands of their understandably livid dad because Paul yet again dragged their family through a slimy pit of yuck in front of the whole small town of Rock Creek.

She'd reinvented life for herself. A life of her very own, without a trace of Paul's shadow. Now in her final year at Baylor, and on track to graduate that spring, she no longer felt twisted up inside about what she should do or shouldn't do and wondering when she'd get the chance to be whoever it was bundled up inside, waiting to emerge. College had been her cocoon. Her metamorphosis.

Now? She had her own wings.

"Look. There's history." She caught Janelle's smirk. "It's not what you're thinking, okay? Just know, Tommy is nice. Comes off shy. He's good looking. And he's a total player. You're coming to make sure I don't lose myself in all of Paul and Tommy's everlasting junk. That's what I'm asking—begging—you for here."

"Mmm." The smile faded from Janelle's face, and she nodded. "Bring you back alive."

"No. Don't let me forget that *I have a life*. And it isn't theirs."

Janelle sobered. "Then it's really serious."

Dre dared eye contact and blinked, irritated that the liquid beneath her lids burned. Disappointment had a way of doing that. Making her more emotional than she'd rather claim to be. And when it came to both Paul and Tommy, disappointment wasn't even the right word. Texas had become not only her new starting point but her refuge. Unfortunately, she had a nauseating feeling that up north in the familiar bearings of her childhood, with the boys sitting across from her, she'd be prone to forget her metamorphosis.

"I'm in." Janelle's fingers curled over Dre's and squeezed.

Dre released a long, quiet sigh. Paul and Tommy could be anything they wanted to be. Didn't matter to her. At the end of the break, she was coming back.

Without either of them shadowing her new life.

***

Three words. That was all it'd taken to strip off rational thinking. Tom was pretty sure that qualified him as insane. Straight-up, not-anywhere-near-right-in-the-head crazy.

Dre's coming home.

Paul had dropped those loaded syllables without any kind of pretense or understanding as to how that would mess with Tom. How could he know? Though Tom would forever claim Paul as his buddy and closest friend, the fact was, Paul had spent most of the previous decade wrapped up in himself and the destruction he'd found without even trying. He was clueless about some things. Sometimes, that burned. Other times...

Not so much.

Dre, however. She was never clueless. About anything. Innocent? Yes, and thank God for that—because it was no thanks to Paul or himself. Ignorant? Nope. Dre knew so much more than she let on, which was likely why she'd left and apparently had no intention of coming back.

Tom stared out his window as the sunset lit the rolling winter prairie with an orange-and-pink haze. Hadn't seen many sunsets that didn't make him think of her. She loved them. Would stop, even as a kid, to watch the horizon light up with the evening show.

Dre was coming home for Thanksgiving. One solid week of his best friend's sister. A girl Tom had watched grow up. Teased alongside her older brother. Walked beside while trying to figure out what to do with the rebel Paul had become. And secretly...

Well. She'd grown pretty. And kind. And she'd always been smart.

And always, Paul's little sister. Tom hadn't had the guts to test that dynamic. So he'd found other ways—girls—to keep himself distracted, which proved to be a stupid plan.

That right there was enough reason for him to head on

south to his grandfather's farm in Kansas and join the regular family Turkey Day gathering. As if he should have needed a reason to do that anyway. He'd always had a knack for knowing what to do and then *not* doing it. Or knowing what shouldn't be done and ignoring that wisdom.

Tom rubbed his cheek. Even against his calloused, work-worn palm, the bristles of his two-day beard scratched. The skin on his jawline beneath his hand burned. As if she'd just slapped him.

How could a five-year-old memory be that fresh?

She was coming home. He had every reason not to be there for that long-awaited event. Didn't need an excuse. Didn't even need to say where he would be. Kansas. With his family. Obviously. And yet.

Think your family would mind one more at the Rustin Thanksgiving table? It's not the same in Kansas…

His heart had raced while those words dumped out of his mouth two days before. Unbidden. Unfiltered.

Paul had shrugged. Smacked his shoulder. Completely oblivious, because while Paul was on track to a full one-eighty, there were some things he still didn't see. Probably because Tom had kept them pretty tight to himself. And Dre hadn't been back much in the four years since she'd left for Baylor.

You know you're always welcome, Paul had said. Part of the family, buddy.

That sealed it. Dre was coming home.

And for better or worse, Tom was going to be right there in the Rustin home to see her. The spot on his face where palm had met flesh still stung.

Worse was a really strong possibility.

Chapter Two

CONCENTRATING ON THE DESIGN PROGRAM HAD NEVER BEEN AN ISSUE.

This had been her jam. Was still her jam, bless it. Except, she couldn't keep the reel in her mind set on *Advanced Interior Design: From Conception to Reveal.*

Because.

He'll be there. Why is he going to be there? For the love! His family moved, so why is he going to be with her family for Thanksgiving?

For the love, indeed. This was her favorite class, and she was caught up in the stupid Tommy Kent situation waiting at home, instead of perfecting her kitchen design. This project could launch her to the top of her class. Give her an edge on the projects coming up next semester. She could be assigned point on them, allowing her almost full creative control. Distinguishing her among the other students, who were now bent over their computers in the class.

But there she was. Stewing. Not focusing.

For. The. Love.

This was why she'd begged Janelle to go with her. She hadn't even left the warm Texas soil yet, and Tommy Kent was wrecking her. As if he even had the right. A dust devil of anger vibrated in her chest.

Why on earth was he staying in Rock Creek?

Better question. Why in all of heaven's glory did she care? *This* was her home. Texas. A perfectly inconvenient thirteen-hour drive from her little Nebraska hometown—that, note it carefully in bold Sharpie ink—*was no longer* her hometown.

"I expect functional perfection and jaw-dropping creative beauty." Tami Cooper, her professor and owner of the impressive Live Oak Design, stood from her desk at the front, signaling the end of class. "Remember to use your break wisely. And also, Happy Thanksgiving. Travel safely."

Chairs scraped against linoleum, and laptops clicked shut. That was a wrap, and all that remained was to toss her bag into her Camry's trunk, alongside Janelle's, and head north. Dre ignored the fact that alongside the strong throb of dread, and irritation that she should have to dread going home, was also a pronounced and undeniable sliver of something else entirely.

Not. Excitement.

Maybe excitement. She was going to see her family, for all that was good and happy. And Mama had said Paul was doing well. Really well. Something to seriously be excited about, because five years ago she was pretty sure he'd be a resident in some kind of correctional facility by now.

Excitement, placed correctly, was acceptable.

"Andrea Rustin."

Tami Cooper stopped her as she neared the door, jarring her out of her mental redirective pep talk.

Dre turned, a professional smile anchored on her mouth. "Yes, ma'am?"

Mrs. Cooper returned the grin, kindness in her eyes. "I wanted to let you know how impressed I've been with your work." She put a hand to Dre's arm and squeezed. "You're aware that teaching is a part-time gig for me, right?"

"I've heard something like that." Dre's heart did a little hop-pound-hop routine in her chest, anticipating an exciting direction for this conversation. Everyone knew Tami Cooper had been a breakout designer. Her success with Live Oak Design had allowed her to launch her own line of decorative home goods that was garnering attention beyond the Texas borders. She had a reputation for perfection that blended uniquely with her reputation for kindness, and everyone in Dre's design class held out a secret hope that Mrs. Cooper would tap their shoulder next.

Mrs. Cooper nodded. "My other job is much more hands on. And I'm always on the lookout for real talent. You, my young friend, have real talent."

That professional smile Dre fought to maintain morphed into the kind you'd expect from a ten-year-old at Disney World, which was a little embarrassing but impossible to tame. "Thank you, ma'am."

With another squeeze on Dre's arm, Ms. Cooper nodded again and stepped away. "Have a good break, Ms. Rustin. I look forward to seeing what you've done with this assignment when you get back."

The hippity-hoppity heart thing stammered while her Disney-experience smile melted. That was it? Dre stepped into the hall and moved down the corridor, ruminating over the entire ten-second conversation.

It? No, that was something. Big. A little bait. Motivation. Keep working hard. Keep focus.

"Andrea."

Now near the exit, Dre stopped cold and turned again. "Yeah?"

"Your best asset isn't your talent." Mrs. Cooper stepped closer, her eyes trained on Dre's. "Don't get me wrong. Your talent is significant, as is your work ethic, I might add. But what makes you stand out is who you are with people. You have a warmth and a humor and a genuineness that will make you successful *in life*, no matter what you choose to do or where you end up. Hold on to that."

"Oh." That was a serious compliment. Like, ranking among the best possible ever. Yet Dre wasn't sure what to make of it. Was Mrs. Cooper still insinuating that she might have a job for her after graduation? Or was this a "good luck, kid" pep talk that a professor would give as they pushed a student out the door?

Dre licked her lips and found that professional smile again. "Thanks."

Ms. Cooper stalled, her pause thoughtful and intentional, and then unexpectedly, the woman stepped closer and wrapped an arm around Dre's shoulders. As she tugged her into a kind hug, she said, "I don't know why, but I felt compelled by God to say that to you. I try to follow Jesus, and when He says to speak, I do it. Even if it doesn't make sense."

Warmth spiraled with a massive dose of bewilderment. That was a first. Of ever. No one Dre knew talked like that, did things like that. And she'd been a Christian since the ripe old age of six.

"Have a good trip home, Andrea."

"Oh." Dre shook off the muddle of confusion and met Ms. Cooper's look. "Yeah, thanks. Hope you have a good break too."

It was miles down the road, with Point of Grace belting out *I'll Be Believing* because she was feeling a little bit nostalgic about her music choices, before the truth hit her. Janelle matched the lead singer's powerful melody with impressive force and accuracy, when Dre realized something profoundly significant.

Mrs. Cooper told her to have a good trip home. And Dre hadn't mentally corrected her about the *home* thing. Didn't even think about it. Because in her mind, she was smiling, excited for the first time in years to go back home.

Even if Tommy Kent would be there.

***

"I'm going to need you to prep me on your family situation a little bit better." Janelle settled back into the driver's seat as the Camry gained speed on the highway, the rest stop where they'd switched seats now a distant dot on the horizon at their backs. Janelle had slept for a little more than an hour, allowing Dre an opportunity to ponder going home and what it meant that she had so easily reverted to the idea of this trip as actually *going home.*

It meant that she missed her mama. And her stern but mush-in-the-middle daddy. It meant that there were some really good things about Rock Creek that she'd never get over.

And her brother.

She missed Paul. The Paul of their childhood, who'd had a way of quiet kindness and a fierce protection of her. Like when he'd stood up to Chuck Stanton when the boys were ten because Chuck had slimed her hair with green Jell-O in the cafeteria. Or when she'd been ten and Paul was twelve, he'd silently broke his giant Hershey Symphony bar in half, slipping her one part because she'd left hers in the pickup and it had melted into the bottom of the paper sack. Things any little sister would miss.

Feeling Janelle's glance after her long, silent contemplation, Dre cleared her throat. "Honestly, I haven't seen them much in the last few years, so most of what I've got is history."

"Okay, so give me some history."

Fair enough. Dre knew Janelle's family history, and it definitely wasn't white gloved. "Well, there's my mama. She's a little bit of Aunt Bea from *Andy Griffith*—except far from clueless. She's happy and homey and loving. And then Daddy. He can come off as gruff, but I'm his girl." Dre sent a wink over to Janelle.

"I knew it. Total daddy's girl. Of you and your brother,

you're his favorite, right?"

"Well..."

Sometimes. Yeah, she was. But that wasn't really a favoritism thing. Really. It was an ease thing.

Those happy childhood days for Paul and Dre hadn't lasted into their teenage years, because past age fourteen, Paul had found himself in trouble more often than not. Which meant he was too busy ducking for cover from whatever idiotic prank or illegal activity he'd been messing with. That made their dad more stern than mush for a lot of years. Made her mama worry almost constantly.

"Let's just say that my brother gave me a front-row seat to the after-school special called *How to Mess Up Your Life and Everyone You Care About in Ten Destructive Steps*, starring none other than Paul Rustin." Dre swallowed against the lingering disappointment. "I was the easier kid. Didn't get into much trouble. Liked walking a straight line. Which kept my relationship with my parents pretty calm."

Paul's relationship with their parents had been anything but calm.

But he was her brother. Always her brother. And she found herself equal parts scared that she'd find him dead in a rolled-over pickup somewhere on the highway due to driving while intoxicated, and furious that somehow he'd forgotten who he was or decided being that kid wasn't interesting enough for him anymore.

She hadn't wanted to creep a toe down that same path. While trying to do whatever she could to make sure Paul didn't actually kill himself, Dre made dang sure she wasn't walking through the gate of his destination. She'd worked her tail off getting good grades. Made sure she was respectful to and also had the respect of her teachers. Pretty much worked to be everything opposite of what Paul had become.

Her efforts bore fruit. Turned out straight A's, a decent ACT score, and some pretty high praise in the form of letters of recommendation had the combined power to land some significant scholarships. She'd had many options—several of them within her home state—but by the time her senior year had rolled around, Dre was certain she needed to leave.

Not all of that had to do with Paul. A lot of it. But not all.

Dre sighed, her eyes unfocused on the blurring landscape zipping past her window. "Bottom line: Paul made life chaos. So if I was the preferred kid, that was the only reason."

"Is he still finding trouble?"

Her stomach clenched a little. Guilt, most likely. She'd kind of given up on him. Stopped checking in with him. Moving forward with life was easier that way. "Mama says he's doing better. He's living at my grandparents' ranch now, so I sure hope he's not being stupid out there with them."

"That's good." Janelle tipped back her bottled water, capped it with an awkward hands-on-steering-wheel-while-applying-a-lid move, and returned the bottle to the cup holder between them. "What about this Tommy guy? What's his role in all that drama?"

In the midst of that story—the one where her big brother played the part of hero to her little-girl self, the one that then turned to fearful disappointment in that hero—there had been Tommy Kent. A near constant in all of it, though rarely center stage. Pinning down his role in that saga was actually difficult.

When she was little, he'd been a lot like Paul. The big brother protector. But sometimes the antagonist too. Others, the includer—the one who invited her to play catch in the backyard. Climb the trees near the creek at his family's hobby farm outside of town. Sometimes to go out to eat with them at Ms. May's, once she was in high school.

The transition into teenage life had been awkward between her and Tommy. That was really all she could pin down. That, and he turned out to be almost as much of a disappointment as

Paul.

Maybe for her, more so.

"Dre?"

"Yeah." She straightened, cleared her throat, and tried to push away the ache of something she didn't really understand but was pretty sure didn't belong within her heart.

"He was your childhood crush, wasn't he?" Janelle's tone was all teasing.

It didn't feel funny. Should have, and Dre wanted with all of her self-preserving dignity to laugh the truth of it off, push Janelle's shoulder, and tell her those things were silly and so very little girl. But the little girl inside her screamed not to belittle her heart. And the woman closer to the surface didn't want to own that maybe that little-girl crush had never been outgrown.

The teasing smile faded from Janelle's lips. "Maybe not just childhood, huh?"

Dre fingered the frayed yarn at the cuff of her sweater, milling through screaming thoughts and memories for a response that wouldn't force her to say things she didn't want to admit.

"He was always there. And was usually really nice." Swelling in her throat cut her thoughts right there.

"Usually."

Dre picked a memory. One that wasn't uncommon in the last year of Tommy's high school career. A pretty girl sitting on his lap, arms wound around his neck. In that particular memory, it had been Abigail Nicks—senior, cheerleader, and quite the talker. Didn't have one single secret about her whole life. Including Tommy Kent. There were other options to choose from—Candi Stalts, Amy Yultz, Melissa Short. Dre focused on Abigail, though, because Abigail told all, confirming what Dre had suspected.

Disgust smothered the quiet ache Dre hadn't wanted there

in the first place.

"He's nice. And a player. We've already been over this." Dre snagged the water bottle from her cup holder and chugged.

"And you're not bitter about that at all."

"Nope." She wiped her lips and replaced the bottle. "It was only a childhood crush."

Which meant nothing. Clearly.

Nothing at all.

***

Good sense settled into Tom's bones somewhere around one in the morning. Strange, since sleep deprivation usually had the opposite effect. But after several nights of not sleeping well—that one particularly brutal because Dre's bright-blue eyes and unforgettably soft hair made him twitchy—solid good sense paid him a visit.

The solution was surprisingly simple. And really not much of a shocker.

Leave.

Don't be in Rock Creek when she got back.

That should do it. Return normal sleeping patterns, for starters. And then, maybe normal life. Such as it was.

So Tom tossed a few plaid button-downs, a good pair of jeans and a work pair of jeans, and enough clean socks and underwear for a week into his old gym duffel. Over a shared morning cup of coffee in Paul's grandma's kitchen, which had become routine since Tom had become an added ranch hand to the Rustin spread south of town, he told Paul he'd changed his mind and was gonna do Turkey Day with the family in Kansas.

"Okay," Paul had said, a mild scowl creasing between his eyes. "But I was planning on you helping sort down on the river property Wednesday."

Wednesday was only five days away. Would allow easy time to get down to the Kansas spread, because from the river property, Tom's grandparents' place was only a three-hour drive south. Still. Wednesday was five whole days away. That would be five whole days of insanity, because Dre was due to roll into town that afternoon.

Tom couldn't afford any more sleepless nights. And he really couldn't do any more silent madness.

"Sorry, buddy. I'm gonna have to bow out this time."

Paul gulped down the rest of his joe, looked at Tom squarely, and tipped an odd expression. "You're not right these days. You know that?"

Paul had no idea.

"Just...feeling guilty. It being a holiday and all."

"In five days."

"Right."

Paul hit him with another crazy-guy stare and then shook his head. "Right. You working today, or are you extending your *holiday* further still?"

"Let's get to it already."

Paul grunted. The unimpressed, but whatever sort.

So they worked. Fed cattle. Checked fence in the east pasture. Repaired a windmill that had gone caput sometime the week before.

The cold fog refused to clear that day, which seemed ironic since clarity had finally settled in Tom's mind. By the end of the day he was damp on every surface and chilled clean through. But he waved off Grandma Rustin's offer of hot soup and homemade bread—an honest-to-goodness sacrifice— saying he needed to hit the road. Which he did. Immediately.

There was one stoplight in town. Only one, right in the middle, directly past the only fill station in Rock Creek. It happened to be red when he reached it. And there happened to be one other car at the lit-up intersection, directly across from him. And the vehicle happened to be a dark-blue Toyota Camry.

The driver, familiar enough to make out in the glow of streetlights, happened to have a pair of blue eyes. The same exact shade that had been waiting behind his eyelids all week, keeping him from sleep.

Turned out, his brain was still every bit as foggy as the Rustin ranch had been all day, because it only took one look. Her stare connected with his.

That was it.

Good sense was gone.

Chapter Three

"MORNING, BUMPKIN-GIRL."

Mama grinned, holding out a cup of coffee while Dre shuffled into the kitchen.

Dre's mouth stretched into a sleepy smile. Yeah. She'd missed her mama. "Morning." She leaned in, simultaneously accepting the mug and landing a peck on Mama's soft cheek.

Mama gathered Dre around the waist and squeezed. "Oh, how I miss my girl."

"Miss you too, Mama."

One more squeeze, and Mama stepped away, nodding to the breakfast table nestled in the crowded kitchen. Janelle slept soundly in Dre's room. Not surprising. The woman would be happy to sleep until noon if no one bothered her.

Dre's mind slipped into creative mode, and she shuffled the features of her family's kitchen, rearranging, considering better functional options...

"I'd love to see it on paper." Mama slipped into a chair across from the one Dre had landed in.

"What's that?"

"The design you're creating right now. It's for this"—she waved over the area that was long overdue for an update—"right?"

Dre chuckled quietly. "You always could read me."

"Not such a bad thing."

"No. Not a bad thing at all." Dre sipped her coffee, spiked with vanilla cream. The taste made her heart warm—Mama drank her coffee black, and Daddy didn't drink it at all. The creamer had been purchased for her.

"Been missing my girl." A warm work-worn hand covered Dre's. "Wondering if she'd ever come home."

"I'm sorry, Mama."

"Now, I wasn't fishing for an apology. I raised you to go out and live, even if that's not here. No guilt from you for that. Just wanted you to know that you're missed."

Liquid burned in her eyes. How could it have been possible that homesickness had rarely plagued her while she was in Texas, but now, sitting right there in her childhood home, the ache for it grew heavy?

Inhaling and savoring the aroma of coffee and Mama's cinnamon coffee cake, she slipped her eyes shut and allowed the feeling of home a moment to settle. Memories of riding bikes down the street, trick-or-treating with the boys, and playing tag at Settler's Park in the middle of town drifted through her mind. And then paused.

The park in Rock Creek held a special place with her, though she'd never even realized it. It had been built around a big old barn that was now a historical landmark, making the place stand out as unique. As the little girl in her mind ran around, yelling, laughing, the setting she was in came into focus, and more scenes rolled through her memory. Warm summer nights, when the sun took its sweet time to bid good night, they'd tossed a football over the soft green grass with the old barn marking the out-of-bounds boundary. Leaves on the ash trees turning bright yellow in the fall, making a stunning backdrop for that same old barn. Snow piling in drifts around the thick, weathered siding of that giant old beauty...

That barn. Man, she might love that barn. Someone really

ought to make it special.

"How's life down there?" Mama asked.

Jolted back to the present in her mama's kitchen, Dre looked up. "It's good." She swallowed, fighting to ignore the contradiction and uncomfortable emotions that had been disturbed. Being homesick wasn't normal for her, and why on earth had she suddenly become fixated on Rock Creek's park for no reason whatsoever?

"And school?"

"Really good. I'm near the top of my class, and my design professor is amazing. She kind of hinted that she might have something for me after I graduate. Maybe even sooner."

Mama's smile beamed pride. "I'm not surprised."

A spell of silence drifted between them, and Dre fingered the handle of her coffee mug.

"How about that young man you're seeing. Cameron? How is he?"

Dre met Mama's eyes. Hadn't she told her? "Cameron and I decided we weren't a good fit. We broke up in August, before school started up again."

"You did?"

"Yeah. I thought I said something to you about it."

"Hmm." The space above Mama's nose wrinkled. "I don't remember that. In fact, I was surprised you weren't bringing him with you when you said you were coming home. But maybe I forgot."

Mama forget important things like that? Not likely. More likely Dre failed to bring it up. Had she really lost touch that much?

"Are you okay with it?" Mama touched her arm, the contact gentle and warm. "With the breakup, I mean. Was it hard?"

Stuck in a bewilderment at her own detachment, Dre studied her mother. How had that happened? Seriously. She and Mama had been close. She'd told her mother about all her crushes as a kid—well, except one. The big one. But still. She didn't typically keep things from Mama. Hadn't kept this thing either. Not intentionally.

"Oh, honey..." Mama stood, anchoring a strong arm around Dre's shoulders.

"No, it wasn't hard. We agreed that it wasn't love for either of us, and we're still friends." Dre blinked. A couple of tears escaped anyway.

"But you're crying."

"I can't believe I didn't tell you." A sob surged forward, repressed emotion Dre hadn't realized she'd blocked away. "I can't believe it's been so long since I've been home. I can't believe how much I don't talk to you anymore. How did this happen?"

A pinprick jabbed into the sudden ache, sharp and decisive. It felt like...anger? Yes. Anger. And it was focused on Paul.

And Tommy.

If she'd been avoiding home, it was because of them.

The bang of a car door cracked through the quiet of the house. Followed by a second. Dre wiped the pool of moisture from her eyes, and Mama squeezed her with both arms.

"That'll be Paul." Mama stood, then paused, a look of puzzlement on her face. "Thought Tommy had decided to go to Kansas after all. But there were two door slams. Weren't there?"

Yes. Two. Paul's, then Tommy's, for certain. "I saw Tommy in town last night on my way home."

"You did? Paul called yesterday and said Tommy changed his mind."

The rumble of voices floated past the front door, along with the scuffled sound of boots being wiped on the welcome mat. The voices were as easily recognized as her own. Deep banter. A chuckle she knew well.

"Sounds like he changed his mind again." Dre kept her tone

detached. Only mildly interested.

Mama pinned a look on her—warm but knowing. A spiral of unease filled Dre's middle.

Apparently Mama had known about *the big one*, whether Dre had told her or not. And by the breath Mama held, Dre wondered what other things the woman knew.

***

This was normal. Tom had walked into this house eighty million times before. Had seen that cute blonde in her sweats, hair whipped up in that beautiful mess she often did, face clean of makeup, and a coffee mug in her hand one hundred times at least.

Normal shouldn't feel like this. Chest pain and shortness of breath weren't on the symptom list for *normal.*

Paul stepped forward from their position inside the door, not a glance toward Tom. Thank heaven. Meant he hadn't noticed the fact that Tom stopped breathing and had suddenly developed a staring problem.

"There's my beautiful little sister."

There was nothing patronizing in Paul's voice at all. Apparently Dre heard the mix of humility and sincerity, because the corners of her mouth peaked while her eyes brimmed with joy. At Paul. Which was a relief. The last time Tom had seen the pair of siblings together, Dre could barely look at Paul, and when she did, the look was one of total frustration, not love.

This look was all love.

"Paul." Her voice wavered a bit as she collided into his chest. Paul wrapped her up tight and held on.

Few knew what this moment really meant to his best friend. But Tom did. Paul had come to a thawing season, and with it he'd unearthed a great pile of regret. Dre was among the damaged rubble, and Paul had told Tom that he was afraid he'd never get the chance to show Dre how sorry he was. How much his heart had changed.

"She doesn't answer my calls, Tom," he'd confided once, desperate sorrow thick in his voice. "And the few times I've actually talked to her and not to her voicemail, she cuts me short. Says she's busy."

Hadn't sounded like the Dre Tom had known. Then again, he and Paul had both pushed too far. He could hardly blame her for wanting to move on.

"You look great, kid." A smile coated Paul's voice as he stepped back, holding Dre at arm's length. "Really great. Life been good?"

"Yeah." She smiled. A beautiful grin that just about carved Tom in two.

She was happy. In Texas, with her life. She deserved to be happy. What was he doing here?

Her gaze shifted from Paul to Tom, and the moment he connected with those familiar eyes, he remembered exactly why he was there.

Her. He needed to see her. Even if it meant that at the end of the week he'd tell her goodbye forever, at least it wouldn't be like the last goodbye. He couldn't live with the last goodbye, and he didn't want her to either.

"Hi, Tommy."

His mouth twitched. *She still calls me Tommy.* That had to be good, right? Because the last time he'd seen her, the conversation ended with something like, *Hope you can live with your mistakes, Thomas. I'm not going to be one of them.*

"Hey, Dre." He slid a half step forward, uncertainty tilting his world. "It's good to see you."

She stood mute. Tom could feel Paul and Mrs. Rustin watching. Waiting. Wondering... But he couldn't move forward, and he couldn't look away. He could only stand, wait for her move. Hope that in the four years since she'd left, he'd actually grown up the way he would have sworn yesterday he had, and that she hadn't completely smothered the place in her heart that had admired him.

Her smile faded, and a cloud passed over her expression. But the moment the heart in his chest sagged, she moved forward, closed the space between them, and slid tentative arms over his shoulders.

He tucked his mouth against her shoulder as he circled her waist, hoping the fabric of her hoodie would muffle his sigh.

"Do I smell cinnamon rolls, Mom?" Paul turned into the kitchen, away from Tom and Dre, and a quick glance told Tom that Paul had slung an arm around his mom and was walking with her toward the oven.

Tom tightened his hold. Dre leaned away, palms first on his shoulders, and then her touch gone completely. She glanced toward the ground, and heat danced red across her cheeks. The space between them felt like torture, and her silence shouted rejection.

She swallowed. He could actually hear it. "Paul said you were going to be here."

A statement that was a question. Did he have to answer it honestly?

"Yeah."

That was...pathetic.

She lifted her face, met his eyes with a challenge.

"I called you a couple of times," he said. A fact he'd omitted in the few conversations he and Paul had that involved Dre.

"I know."

"You didn't call me back."

Her posture became rigid. "Did you need something?"

He stuffed his shaking hands into his coat pocket. "Yeah. I needed to talk to you. Have some things to say."

"Think we've already said all the words we need to say to each other."

The left side of his face burned, the edges of the heat the shape of her hand. As if she'd slapped him. Again.

He swallowed. Looked at his boots. Her socked feet. The fists she'd rolled at her sides. The jaw she'd clenched. Her eyes, lit with blue heat.

"Dre—"

"Morning, early risers of Nebraska. Did y'all know it's as cold as a frosted frog up here in this country?" A female voice overrode his from the hall at his back. Whoever was behind him sniffed long and loud. "Mmm-mh! Something smells devine! Dre, if this is normal, sign me up for every holiday break. Fatten me up with some cinnamon goodness, and I'll survive this arctic climate."

Dre took a decisive step backward, stuffed her hands into the kangaroo pocket of her sweatshirt, and brushed up a grin that was nearly convincing. "Morning, Janelle. Come meet my brother. And his friend Tom."

Her brother. And her brother's friend. Tom.

Tom wondered what he'd expected. And why this gutshot hadn't been it.

***

"Something you want to tell me?" Paul barely had the door to his pickup shut before he drilled that question.

Though he could feel his eyebrows rise, Tom didn't look at Paul. "You need a haircut?"

"Nice." Paul jammed the keys into the ignition but didn't turn the engine over. "Try again."

"Okay. What do you want to know?"

"I want to know why that reunion with my sister this morning turned suddenly intense and not exactly happy."

Wasn't getting out of it then. Tom had held out a reasonable hope Paul wouldn't bring it up. After all, Paul had been the one to guide his mom out of the room when that *good to see you* hug lasted a little bit long. And Paul had been all charm and ease while they'd chatted the morning away with his parents, Dre, and Dre's quirky friend, Janelle. Seemed like maybe Paul was going to keep his nose on his face, which would be convenient right now.

Paul turned, fingers pulled into a fist, and leaned toward Tom. "What did you do to my sister?"

Of all the hypocrisy. Did Paul know how many times he'd run over his own sister? How often she'd been humiliated because of something stupid and selfish Paul had said or done? Did he even realize that he'd put his little sister in harm's way because she'd felt like she needed to somehow keep him alive and unbroken? She'd pulled him out of fist fights. Wrestled him for the keys to his pickup when he was drunk. Gone looking for him in places and at times that nice girls really shouldn't.

With a spike of irritation, Tom shoved Paul's shoulder back. "Nothing."

After a good hard look, Paul shook his head. "Lying was always more my thing than yours. Don't start up with it now."

"Yeah, well, blameless isn't really something you can claim, and I've had to protect her from you more than once, so knock off the self-righteous act. I'd never hurt Dre, and you know it. And that's all you need to know."

Paul hesitated another three seconds, his look pinned on Tom with a mix of concern and confusion. Then he turned back to the ignition, and they started on their way back to his grandparents' place fifteen miles down a country road. Paul kept quiet most of the drive, though by the working of his jaw, the occasional rubbing of his chin, and a few more glances toward Tom than Tom was comfortable with, it was easy to assume Paul wasn't done with the subject.

They pulled into the drive as Pops strode from the barn

toward the Rustins' old farmhouse. Right on time for Pop's lunch break, during which he'd instruct them both on which fence needed checking that afternoon and how to fix the inevitable sagging section that they'd find. For the one hundred and fiftieth time, at least.

Tom reached for the door handle to make his escape.

"Look."

Dang. No escape.

"I know I've been an idiot. I know that I've been pretty wrapped up with me for a long time. There are things that I've missed. Clearly." He turned a serious stare toward Tom. "But there's no way I'm letting this go, because that was an intense few moments back there, and all of a sudden I'm wondering why you stayed here instead of going to Kansas for Thanksgiving with your family. All of a sudden I'm realizing how very few dates you've been on recently. All of a sudden I'm wondering if Dre's not coming home over the past four years had to do with someone besides me. Things are adding up in this small head of mine, and I'm asking you to be honest."

Tom clamped his molars together. Stared out the window.

"Tom, you're my best friend. Have been forever. If there's something between you and Dre, then say it."

"There's nothing." Liar. Well, not exactly. There wasn't anything between them. Never had been, officially. He blew out a breath. "There's nothing, because I messed up."

"When?"

Did Paul want dates of the offenses she'd certainly lay before him? Details? It was too complicated, and frankly, humiliating to explain.

"Just...a while back, and even then, there was nothing...understood between us. Just. Something...undefined. I don't know. And yes, I stayed because I wanted to see her. Talk to her."

Paul's lips pressed, and he nodded. "Because whatever that

undefined thing was, it's not over?"

Tom could only hope.

Chapter Four

"So that wasn't too awkward."

Janelle belly-flopped onto Dre's double bed, stare fixed with rapt interest on Dre. "And you're right. Tom's nice. Really nice. Not to mention—de-licious." She whistled, a shrill, girly whistle that usually would have made Dre laugh. "Hotter than a burnin' stump."

Dre rolled her eyes. "He's not delicious."

"No, right, that wasn't what you said." She perched up on her elbows and tipped her head with *a look*. "What was it you said? Hmm...something like *crazy good looking with a side helping of knows it*. Did I get it?"

Lifting the magazine she had spread on her lap, Dre worked to ignore her friend.

"Definitely good looking. I'm guessing even better than high school Tommy Kent." Janelle paused. For dramatic effect, certainly. "Didn't pick up on the *knows it* part though."

Dre turned a page, not seeing anything printed on the slick paper.

"He seemed pretty humble actually."

Another page flip.

"And quiet. Didn't have a whole lot to say."

She came to a folded page—one of those perfume sample ads. Unfolding it, she lifted the magazine to take a whiff. Yuck. The strength of the floral smell pierced her head and made her eyes water.

"Maybe he couldn't speak because he was too busy snitching glances at you. Wishing you'd feed his starving soul just one little beatific smile."

That did it. Dre slapped the magazine down onto her stretched-out legs. "Stop. This is not why you're here, remember?"

Janelle's dark eyebrows lifted, and all teasing evaporated, replaced with a stern look. "He very obviously adores you, Dre. Most of us regular girls dream of a man looking at us with that kind of painful longing in his eyes. And he's kept that kind of fire going for years while you've been gone? Come on, girl. Are you sure you know what you're running from?"

The room seemed to move. Her brain felt fuzzy and body buzzed with a tipsy sensation. Probably from the obnoxious perfume she'd inhaled. Squeezing her eyes shut, Dre searched for stability. Instead, she found the image of that very look Janelle had teased her about coming from the face of a man who was definitely—and unfairly—more handsome than the high school version of himself.

She mentally swiped at the image only to have it replaced by the ghost sensation of his arms tightening around her, his sigh sinking hot against her shoulder.

For the love.

She growled. Literally growled out loud right there in front of her friend, who was not currently being what she wanted her to be. "Look, you were here on specific orders. Get me back to Texas. Don't let me forget that I have a life there. Not here."

"Why would I do that when I saw what I just saw?"

"Because you're my friend."

"I'm being your friend. Right now. Like this. So unless you've got a real reason you want to share with the class as to why you're flat-out sprinting from what appears to be a decent guy, this is the new deal: You give him a real chance. Give yourself a real chance. Because you might be hiding out in Texas, afraid to fall in love for no good reason at all. And I'm not supporting that kind of nonsense."

***

Tom spent the night letting memories torture him. Because he probably deserved it for being so ridiculously idiotic. Coulda gone to Kansas. Like good sense had told him to.

One memory landed on replay. Five years back, out there in the pasture, by the small pond of old Mr. Harper's place south of town. The *Watering Hole.* Where they shouldn't have been in the first place. Where they often shouldn't have been.

She'd stayed there. By herself. She was as stubborn as her mule-headed brother. There he was again, the scene as fresh as the wintry air bringing in a promise of snow...

Ache and a heaping dose of fear walloped Tom as he caught the silhouette of her form in his headlights. He should have swept her up and plopped her into the cab of his pickup. Would have—certainly—if he hadn't been reduced to basically calf wrestling Paul into the vehicle so he could get his drunk butt home.

But he hadn't made sure about Dre, which was why he'd driven back after dropping Paul off—making sure Paul's parents knew their son was strung out in the basement. And there she was. Alone in the moonlight of a pasture known for parties among those who were into that scene, on a night that had already turned to the earliest hour of morning.

Arms wrapped tight around herself, she turned when the beam of his headlights cloaked her, posture like a T post. Straight, rigid, and cold.

Still mad. Wasn't fair. What choice did Tom have? He was sick to death of watching her rescue Paul—and cover for him. Sick to death of watching Paul flush his life, and take her down with him, in the swirling vortex of selfish chaos.

Leaning toward the dash, trying to make out her expression, he shifted into park and then popped his door open. "Come on, Dre," he called into the chilly night air. "Time to go home."

She stood as if she'd grown roots. "Not with you."

Sighing, he cut the engine, landed on the dried prairie grass, and flung the pickup door shut. He followed the band of glowing yellow to where his headlights drenched her.

"Come on. You know I didn't have a choice."

"Now you grow a conscience."

"What?"

"Where was this noble concern at every other party? Every other prank? Every other fight? You *would* choose this one— the final straw—to step in."

Fingers rolled tight, he leaned toward her, his senses swirling with confused emotions—anger—at Paul, and now Dre, because what the heck? She'd done exactly what he'd done with Paul a dozen times over. Now this? Pity, because she didn't deserve this from her brother, and Paul had landed himself in a place that was going to be painful for everyone.

And then...

The moment he inhaled her minty scent, his sense slid sideways. This attraction...

He'd tamped it down all year. Paul would have either been embarrassingly stupid or unmanageably livid if he'd known how Tom felt about his baby sister. And more importantly, Dre had enough drama to deal with these days.

But there she was. Looking vulnerable even in her anger. He knew why. That had been Paul's last chance. Last week Paul's dad had caught him high in their basement. Said he was out of chances. Mr. Rustin didn't make empty threats, and he'd laid down an ultimatum that Paul had barreled his bullheaded way right past.

Dre's shoulders quivered, and when she sniffed, Tom melted into warm putty. Never mind that she'd accused him of not being there for Paul. Of hauling her brother off to his doom. Of being a bad friend. Watching her heart break dissolved all resentment.

Honestly, sometimes he had been a bad friend. He'd stayed quiet way too long. Stood on the sidelines while Paul became a one-man train wreck.

He'd felt confused and helpless in it all. And also, he had some stuff going on inside that he hadn't gripped yet and didn't want them to know. Especially not Dre. *Surely she didn't…*

Tom hadn't known what to do about it—any of it. So he went with nothing. Watched while the drama of his best friend's choices smothered the girl who tugged at the tender places in his heart.

With two long strides, he closed the space between them. She leaned against his chest the moment his arms closed around her, and the soft sniffles morphed into an all-out sob.

He knew her ache. Shared it. Paul was his best friend, and watching him sabotage his own life—dragging his family through hell with him—was painful. Tom could only imagine the mix of anger and pain Dre was drowning in right then.

The hands that had been flat against his shirt balled into fists, clenching the material. He pulled her in tighter, tucked his face next to hers.

"Dre, this isn't on you or me. Paul's gonna live how he's gonna live. Make his own mistakes. You shouldn't be the one pulling him out of his messes anymore."

"Daddy's going to send him to Omaha," she stammered, her breath ragged from tears.

"I know." Tom rubbed her shoulder, then slid his hand until his thumb found the tense place on her neck. "Paul knew that too. This isn't anyone's fault but his own."

Her cries slowed. Calmed. Yet she stayed tucked against him, like she wanted to be there. Soft in his arms, as if he'd become her refuge. His mind shifted as his body warmed. The ends of her hair brushed the chapped skin of his hand, provoking the memory of its silk between his fingers the time he'd told Paul he needed to learn how to braid a horse's tail and then proceeded to show him how on Dre's hair. That'd been a while back, but his fingers remembered keenly, longed to feel the softness yet again.

He'd liked her a long time.

And there she was, snuggled up against him, hot breath fanning against his chest. Pretty hair begging to be touched. Clean, minty scent making his mind deliciously numb.

Cautiously, he slid forked fingers into the thick mass of shoulder-length blond silk. She moved, but only to dip her forehead into his sternum. Courage and longing both nudged north. With the smallest move away, and a palm sliding from her cheek to her chin, he tipped her face up to his.

Through wide eyes, she watched him while the pad of his thumb slid beneath the line of her bottom lip. When he bent, eliminating the breath of night air between his mouth and hers, she didn't move.

He took her lack of response as shock, not rejection, and the pull of her—this girl he'd known forever and had liked for longer than he'd realized—had him dipping in for another taste.

She responded. Lips moved against his, taking a taste of her own. Trepidation evaporated, and he let his mouth take what he longed for. More of her.

Until she froze.

Hands flat on his chest, she stepped back. While he still fisted the mass of hair he'd woven with tender recklessness between his fingers, she lifted a palm and landed a firm blow just above his jaw.

He jerked straight. "Dre?"

"I'm not Abigail." Breathless hurt resonated in her shaking voice. She took another step back, dislodging her hair from his hand. "Not one bit like her, and don't you dare think otherwise."

The words crushed like another blow as heated shame washed through him. *She knew.* Yeah. They all made their own choices. Mistakes. Some of those, they'd desperately wish back.

With an angry stride, she sidestepped him and moved toward the road.

"Dre, wait." Body cold and shaking, Tom turned and caught her hand.

She pushed him away and glared through sheened eyes.

"You can't walk home," he said. "It's one in the morning."

"All of a sudden you're worried?"

"I've always worried. Always cared."

Her lips pressed tight, but she continued to glare, disgust stamping more heat into his already burning face.

Tom squeezed his eyes shut and sighed. "Just let me take you home, okay?"

She glanced back at the road, and a second later her shoulders slumped. "Fine. But don't talk to me. And definitely don't touch me."

His cheek throbbed, and her sharp silence killed as he drove her back into town. When he pulled up to the curb at the Rustin home, he clicked the gear into park and turned toward Dre.

Staring out the window, she sat motionless. A tear near her nose caught the light of the streetlamp above them, and Tom longed to brush it away with his thumb. To slide over, curve his arms around her, and tell her she could cry. That this hurt she carried, he understood, and he was sorry he'd contributed to it. Disappointed her.

If she only knew... No. She still wouldn't understand. He didn't really understand. What had he been doing? Why?

What was the driving need within that had pushed him?

Really, he didn't have any answers. Nothing that didn't seem pathetically selfish or shallow. But maybe...

Drawing a breath, he summoned courage again. "Dre, can we talk for a minute?" He'd tell her that it wasn't as bad as she thought, and that he was sorry. The last thing he wanted in the world was for her look of contempt to be pinned on him.

She straightened, swiped away the tear, and reached to open the door.

"Please, Dre."

Her boots hit the pavement with a smack, but she turned to face him, anger lighting her eyes. "Hope you can live with *your* mistakes, Thomas Kent. I'm not going to be one of them."

Tom stared at his hands while the sound of her boots against pavement punctured the midnight air.

She'd avoided him the rest of the year. Pummeled him with silence. Froze him with her arctic cold shoulder. Then spent the summer with a cousin on the other side of the state and made sure she wasn't around until after he left for the ag school near his grandparents' farm in Kansas.

The following spring, she graduated. In August, she left, and stayed gone.

Now, these years later, alone in the silence of his small rental in town, the irony of her angry words spoken that night hit him.

He'd made a lot of mistakes that year. Most of them he still didn't understand why—all he knew was that he'd felt a driving loneliness he'd tried to fill. But Dre? She had no idea— even to this day.

She'd become the mistake he regretted most.

Chapter Five

"We are to be a people marked by radical forgiveness. Those wounds that are deepest—they're likely dealt by someone we have loved deeply. Have you forgiven them?"

Dre fought against Pastor Hurst's words, setting up a shield around her heart so that the thrust of them wouldn't penetrate. This was the Sunday before Thanksgiving. Wasn't he supposed to be preaching about being thankful? Wasn't that the standard calendar sermon plan?

"Can you imagine Peter, standing before Jesus, knowing the depth of his own failure? Breathe in that agony for a moment. Live there, in that point of utter soul destruction, knowing you failed the Christ when you'd sworn that you would die for Him. Can you feel that desolation?

"What if, instead of asking him three times over—and please don't miss that significance—'Do you love me,' He'd said, 'We are done'?"

The shield she fought to raise failed. Absolutely crumbled. *We are done.* Was that what she'd felt, how she'd handled the falling out with her brother? With Tom?

Some people were toxic though. Right? Some people you had to be done with. Wasn't there a point when legitimate lines needed drawn?

"Radical forgiveness..."

Ache throbbed deep, and Dre swallowed hard against the lump in her throat. She hoped the burning liquid in her eyes stayed in place as she sat beside Janelle, wishing she could hide—or that she was somewhere else entirely. How was she to sort through the tangled, whirling thoughts messing up her heart and mind while sitting in the middle of church, next to her best friend, who thought Dre had life pretty well put together, listening to a sermon that was surely intended to scribble all over her neat and tidy world?

God, why here? Why now? Couldn't we have worked on this somewhere private? And not when Paul is on my left, Tom right next to him? I can't do this now.

It was bad enough guilt had driven her home, and not desire. The fact that Mama said she missed her—not in a *get home, child, you owe us a flesh-and-blood hello* sort of way, but in a sincere *I miss my daughter* sort of way, which almost made it worse. Now Pastor had seemed divinely intent on...

What?

The service ended with all the smiles and hugging hellos one would expect for a long-overdue homecoming visit. Dre held her inner self in check, muting the argument brewing between the implication left by the sting of the words *radical forgiveness* and the veneer that her being gone had more to do with being happy than anything else. The debate was bound to be fierce and ugly, and she wasn't sure she was ready for the revelation it might unearth.

She distracted herself by catching glimpses of the barn, its weathered gambrel roofline visible past the other buildings and trees between the church and the park. It was a beauty, and the charm of it made her smile.

Apparently her mask of *I'm so glad to be back* proved effective. They made it home—Mama, Daddy, Janelle, and her—sans Paul and Tom, which Dre chose not to give a moment's thought to, lest she face the fact that she was relieved, and that was telling. Sunday dinner proved to be exactly what had lived in her memory—pot roast, carrots, potatoes, gravy, apple salad, and orange Jell-O. They ate. Chatted. Laughed here and there. And then the group amicably broke apart.

An hour later, Dre unzipped the last of the six freezer bags of halved tomatoes and added them to the frozen clumps in the largest of Mama's stew pot. She double-checked her handwritten recipe—one she'd gotten from a young Mennonite girl she'd met at a horse camp as a pimple-faced thirteen-year-old. They'd hit it off then and had remained pen pals for a while, during which Katie had shared with her some time-honored family recipes. This one had been, in Dre's opinion, the best. Sadly, it'd been ages—four years to be exact—since she'd made it.

The secret was homegrown, sunshine-ripened sauce tomatoes, and a shocking amount of onions. Thus, the time since she'd made tomato soup—she hadn't had a garden, and store-bought produce couldn't come close. But Mama had saved some of her garden deliciousness. Bless her for that.

As she pulled out the tin where Mama kept her onions, the front door swished open and then clicked closed. Dre held her breath, listening to the sound of a pair of boots being wiped on the large entry rug. One pair.

Paul was alone then. That was relief sinking in her stomach. Not disappointment. Certainly.

Paul strode into the kitchen, inhaling with a crooked grin. "I smell something..."

Dre turned her head to look at him, a smile in place. "What?"

"Something methinks I haven't had in way too long."

Chuckling, she finished counting out the onions. "What would that be?"

"Dre's homemade tomato soup."

"You're right on that. If I can get these onions quartered without losing a finger. My vision always goes wonky by about onion number three."

Paul laughed. "I won't let you amputate a finger." He picked up a softball-sized onion and started peeling away the papery covering. "Seriously though, my mouth is all drool right now. I've actually dreamed of your soup on cold winter nights."

She snorted. "That's silly. Mama has the recipe. She's got a freezer full of garden tomatoes that she said she didn't have time to can, so I'm not sure what's holding any of you back."

"Wouldn't be the same." He nudged her shoulder. "Where is everyone?"

"Daddy's downstairs watching the game. Mama's taking her Sunday afternoon nap. Janelle has a massive research paper due the Monday we get back, so she's working on it in my room."

"Ah. And my sister's default is tomato soup. Which is awesome."

A weighted quiet settled between them as the outer layers of onions were peeled and Dre prepared Mama's big wooden cutting board and best knife. There was something serious in Paul's posture, in the glances she felt him land on her profile time and again.

"Dre." His fingers stilled, and he leaned a hip against the counter. "If I ask you something, can I have your word you'll give me a straight-up, no-sugar answer?"

Her midsection twisted. "That sounds...loaded."

"Very loaded. But I'm serious. I want you to be honest."

"Um." She blinked, clamped her jaw, and couldn't bring herself to look at him.

He didn't wait. "You've been gone a long time. And that's fine—except, well, maybe it isn't? What I'm saying—asking—is..." He swallowed, turned to grip the counter, and bent to find her eyes. "Am I the reason you never come back?"

Her jaw and cheekbones ached with the force of her bite.

Her vision swam, blurring his white knuckles against the counter, the onions waiting on the board, the knife resting below her splayed fingers.

Why today? Couldn't we be like normal families who never discuss their issues and smile because it's a holiday?

He waited for several more painfully silent heartbeats, but when she didn't reply, he moved again, this time cupping her arm in a gentle grip.

"I think I know the answer. And I understand why." He tugged, and she turned. "I'm sorry, Dre. I'm so sorry I buried you in all my rebellious crap. That you got lost and hurt in it all. I did some really stupid things, and I put you in a hard place with Mom and Dad. Sometimes in a dangerous place. I'm sure I said horrible things. I know I hurt you deeply."

His voice broke, and she finally looked up to find real tears collecting in the curve of his nose.

It undid her. All stoic pretense crashed as her body quivered with quiet cries.

Paul gripped her hand. "I still don't know why I did all the stuff I did, but I feel like you stay gone because of me. I hate that—and I'm so sorry for it. Mostly, I want you to know, things have changed. I'm not the same eighteen-year-old terrorist you knew, and I really hope that somehow you and I can find a way to have a real relationship. You're my sister, and I miss you."

Words remained locked up inside, trapped by too much emotion, but she stepped nearer, nearly crashing into his chest as her arms wrapped him up tight.

Never. Not in a million years. This Paul? He was too much.

His arms clasped around her shoulders, secure and unmoving. Her grown-up brother, holding her while they cried. Wept over bitter memories. Strife that had wrecked their relationship. Had, in fact, driven her away from home.

"I'm really sorry, Dre." His shaky voice rumbled near her ear. "Even if you're happy in Texas—and I can support that—

I'd really like my sister back. Can we try that?"

"Yes." The word was breathed out as if in relief. A long, bundled relief that had been lodged deep. "Yes, I'd like that."

His palm rubbed her shoulder, and then he stepped back, blowing out a sigh. An awkward moment passed, in which he smiled, she returned the silent seal of reconciliation, and they both wiped their eyes.

Motioning to the onions, Paul ushered them past the strain. "These need quartered?"

"Yes."

"If you tell me what that means, I'll do it so you can do something that isn't going to make you cry more."

She laughed. One of those runny-nose, crying-but-not-crying laughs that felt so very good. Healing and beautiful. Then she showed him what a quartered onion looked like, and he set to work on the remaining six while she washed the celery stalks she needed, found the herbs her mother had frozen, and brought the concoction to a delicious simmer.

It smelled like home, and she was happy.

***

An idea had locked in. She couldn't shake it, and the vision for it was as clear and real in her mind as the chair she sat on. More. If they could pull it off, it'd be pretty amazing.

"You know what I think?" Dre grinned, enjoying the gathering of people she loved.

Mama, Daddy, Paul, and Janelle sat around the table, a game of dominoes spread on the surface, dotted tiles interrupted with mugs stained chocolaty brown with cascades of whip trickling over the edges. She'd found a new recipe for homemade hot cocoa—one with a hint of mint—and loved having the opportunity to try it out.

Paul leaned back in his chair, mug in hand, and smirked.

"That you're getting your backside whipped by your much-wiser and better-at-dominoes brother?"

"No. And all results are questionable when it comes to this game. I don't know why you're allowed to keep score. As I recall, you failed your last two years of math."

He cleared his throat, but nothing on his face indicated true offense. "Actually, you'll recall I failed all my classes my senior year. But that had more to do with not showing up than ability."

Janelle's brown eyes widened. Shock. Probably some worry—certainly expecting the promised dysfunction to surface in this moment. Maybe with a slamming of fists. Hot words meant to wound. Dredging up of history not yet forgiven.

Maybe a different time that would have happened. But not now. Not with this grown-up and much different version of Paul.

"I do recall that, now that you mention it," Dre said, a sassy eyebrow raised and palm extended. "So I say surrender the official score pad."

Paul chuckled, shook his head. "Not on your big ol' Texas life, kid. What you don't know is that I passed my GED with exceptional marks, and Pops has me keeping the books at the ranch. I am entirely reliable now." His mouth spread with a grin that was a little more sincere than tease. Like he had hoped Dre would absorb this information and be proud of him.

She was. And she let it show in her smile, in the way she settled her eyes on his with a newfound peace between them. But she said, with crossed arms, "Be that as it may, I still question your trustworthiness. If you win this match, I'm going to demand a recount by a neutral party."

"Good luck reading his handwriting," Daddy said dryly. "What he didn't include is that Pops lets him do the books because he's the only one who could read the scrawl Pops has kept for the past thirty years. Somehow the pair of them managed to write with the same unintelligible scribble that makes sense to only them."

The little gathering broke into laughter. Paul rubbed his neck, good humor lighting his eyes. "Guilty. What was it you were actually thinking, Dre?"

Oh yeah. That was where this nonsense started. Anticipation made her wiggle in the chair.

"That old barn in the middle of the park. The one that the town can't tear down because it's a historical landmark?"

"Oh no." Paul crossed his arms.

"Don't get all worked up. Yet."

Mama cleared her throat, one suspicious eyebrow lifted. "Is this going to cost a fortune?"

"Only in twinkle lights." Dre smiled as if this was the most brilliant idea she'd had in all her twenty-one years. Quite possibly it was. What could be better than twinkle lights on a historic barn in the middle of town? "The building is safe. Completely usable. The town has to maintain its soundness. Why not make it the centerpiece of Rock Creek? I mean, how many towns have an authentic old barn in the middle of their city park? We should totally be dressing it up. Using it."

Daddy sat forward, leaning his arms against the edge of the table. "For?"

"Fun!" Dre smacked her hands on the tabletop. "Beauty. Charm. Memories. It's just sitting right there. Begging to have a life right along with us. Why not?"

All four pairs of eyes fixed on her. She felt the stares, but in her mind, she was already planning. Designing. And falling in love with the vision she saw in her head.

It would be something. Truly something special, setting this sweet little off-the-beaten-road town apart and providing a stage for some fantastic memories to come. Not that she'd necessarily be there for them in the future. Texas was home now.

Right.

A corner of her heart dropped. Dre swallowed, working to mask the emotion that sneaky thought provoked. Her life in Texas was good. She was doing really well, had some awesome opportunities looming in front of her. Besides, just because her future was a good thirteen hours south of the barn in the middle of Rock Creek didn't mean she couldn't contribute something wonderful to the heart of her hometown.

"We'd have to clear it with the city council," Daddy mused, but not without a heavy taste of positivity. He liked the idea. Dre could see it in the dreamer-ish look in his eyes. The one she'd inherited from him.

Paul nodded. "Tom's got an in there with Roger Stanton. Kind of owes my good buddy a favor—or ten. Might not take much more than a phone call, especially if we're willing to donate the lights."

"You think?" Mama grinned, also on board.

Roger owed Tom some favors? And what did that have to do with the city council? Roger had been a sitting fixture on the political group forever, it seemed, but...

Huh. Small-town politics.

Paul stood, the feet of his chair scraping against Mama's pristine hardwood floor. "I'll go make a phone call." He stepped toward the living room, but stopped behind Dre. Settling a palm on her shoulder, he squeezed. "The things we do for you, kid."

She rolled her eyes. "Yeah. I know."

He shook her shoulder, tugged a piece of her loose blond hair, and moved toward the living room, cell phone in hand.

Watching Paul and Dre together, Mama's smile stretched like heaven had peeked through the clouds. Maybe for her, it had. Heaven knew—and so did Dre—that Mama loved them both fiercely, and Dre had no doubt she'd prayed for a reconciliation of her home.

"So what else is rolling inside that creative head of yours, bumpkin?" Mama asked.

"Yeah." Janelle turned an impish grin toward Dre. "And you have a great big barn sitting in the middle of town? Why on earth are y'all hiding all this charm out there in the big wide open somewhere without letting a body know about it?"

"Just sitting right there." Dre nodded. "Waiting to be used for more than high school sports banners and seasonal storage for the city. I mean, what have we been doing with this treasure all this time?" Enthusiasm had a way of gripping Dre, and she little knew how to tame it when the thrill of it grabbed her. A blessing and a curse, because she was always willing to try something new, but that meant she was acquainted with disappointment. Usually she could manage the fall. With most things.

Save one. And he wasn't a thing, and that had nothing to do with anything in that moment. Except Paul was calling him for a favor.

Come on, Tom. Come through.

A tendril of a thought snaked through the beautiful image of a lit-up barn, flanked by people enjoying hot cocoa, carols, and maybe something special. Unique to Rock Creek. A Christmas piñata?

She tried to focus on that—because, yes, that would be fantastic! But the wisp of a thought grew larger. Solid. And demanding.

Tom would come through on this. She didn't doubt it for a moment. And when he did...

She'd owe him.

That didn't sit comfortably. Especially when she realized the discomfort felt more like butterflies than sinking dread.

***

"Dre needs a favor."

Paul's announcement, made via a phone call, ricocheted all sorts of galloping nerves in Tom's gut. Could there, on this planet, be a better answer to his prayer for guidance? Heaven had opened and dropped an early Christmas gift straight into his chapped palms.

In concise words with an almost neutral tone, Paul laid out Dre's hopes for Rock Creek's landmark barn. Tom drank in every word, gripping the opportunity like he was gonna do eight seconds on a bull. It was that good.

Now. If he could manage to not screw it up, that'd be perfect.

"Got it. I'll call Charles. We'll make it happen."

Now to thread together a decent, brief presentation to send Charles and the other council members over email. It'd have to be convincing, as this was completely last minute, and if Dre wanted in on the decorating—which, duh, she obviously did—they were going to have to make a record-breaking twenty-four-hour decision. Unheard of in the realm of politics.

But, Charles Stanton owed him. Not that Tom would blackmail the man with what he knew of his son, Chuck. Just. Well, Charles knew that Tom kept his mouth shut when he could have easily smeared the Stanton campaign for mayor by divulging what he knew of Chuck, Jr. So. This whole Christmas lights on the barn thing was a mild thank-you for not ruining his career.

All that aside, it was a good idea. A really good idea. This town was about community, and what could be more community than a beautiful central feature that would bring them together? Dre was, in fact, brilliant. A fact he already knew.

Tom grinned, imagining the enthusiastic glow on Dre's face as she told Paul her idea. Paul said she'd looked like she was ten years old and making valentines for her classmates all over again. She'd loved that stuff. Never really cared what she came home with, because her satisfaction cup was all filled up in the giving. Making people smile by whatever creative beauty or deliciousness she could come up with was her lifeblood. It was one of the special things about Dre that had kept her memory next to his heart.

He had the opportunity to clear a path for her to do it again. Heaven help him, he was gonna make it happen.

Chapter Six

Six phone calls, five emails, a quick stop over at the gregarious Stanton house on North Main Street, and a visit with the fire marshal.

That was what it took. There were a few caveats—a request for a design plan and action outline—but that was hardly a concern. In fact, it'd give Dre a chance to shine even more, to do what he happened to know she was studying to do. And she'd crush it. Tom couldn't smother his champion grin even if he'd wanted to as he climbed into his pickup, signed permit in hand.

He'd give it to her himself.
Thank you for that.

The rambunctious rhythm of his heart was only outdone by the tightness in his stomach. He couldn't wait to see her delight. The sheen of glee in her eyes. The joy in her smile.

Maybe she'd see him anew.

Maybe this could be a start, and he'd get the chance he'd been praying for these four solid years.

***

Dre's heart sank when she met Tom's eyes. He stood on the other side of the doorway, looking entirely serious and apologetic. Neither good signs for the barn-decorating plan she'd spent half the previous night mapping out on her design program because the idea of it didn't leave a whole lot of room for sleep.

Typical of her. All enthusiasm. Hardly any realistic grounding. The life of a visionary dreamer.

She prepared herself for the impending disappointment with a solid grip on the front door and a mustered-up expression of indifference. "What'd you find out?"

"Find out?" Tom's forehead wrinkled. "Was I supposed to find something out? I was on my way to your grandparents' ranch, and thought I'd stop by to see if you girls wanted a ride."

"Janelle is scared of her stepbrother's beagle. Not sure setting her in a saddle on a fifteen-hand horse so that we can work twelve-hundred-pound cattle is a great idea. Did Paul say we were coming out today?"

He scrunched his face, as if thinking were painful. "Paul called yesterday about something..."

He scratched his whiskered chin, the sound like the slow peeling of Velcro. For some reason, the desire to feel the rough of his stubble on her palm had her nearly reaching.

Sleep deprivation. Had to be the reason, because the urge was stupidly ridiculous.

"Seemed like it was a little important." A hint of a playing smile bowed his mouth. "Hmm."

He was...teasing? All self-control evaporated. Dre flipped the door open wide and posted both hands on her hips. "Tommy Kent, you stop messing with me right now and tell me what the city council said!"

"Oh yeah. That." His grin spread full, and he lifted a piece of paper she hadn't noticed he'd been holding, probably because it'd been hanging out behind his back.

She skimmed the paragraph, her eyes landing on *hereby approves the request to decorate*, and squealed. All emotion and no thought had her leaping, colliding into Tom's chest and arms twisting around his neck. "You did it!"

His low chuckle warmed her as his arms wrapped her waist. "Wasn't a hard task. They liked the idea."

Suddenly the buzzing in her mind wasn't all about the news he'd brought as the sandpapery stubble of his cheeks brushed against her forehead. Shouldn't have thrilled her, yet her arms stayed tangled around him as if that was exactly what they'd been wanting to do since forever. Her heart ached a hard, sweet rhythm as she breathed in the clean, citrusy sent that had marked itself in her memory as *Tommy Kent*.

Tom didn't seem to be in a hurry to let her go either, and though they were still in the open doorway, the November chill heavy with its promise of snow, warmth blanketed her body.

This is Tommy Kent!

Yeah, the boy she'd had a crush on since she was fourteen. The one who could tease her in a way that made her feel special and not flattened. Whose smile was better than a strong cup of coffee alongside a banana chocolate chip muffin.

Tommy Kent, Dre. Who proved himself to be less than she'd believed. Who had also done little to nothing to keep Paul out of trouble until the last straw, leaving her frustrated and feeling alone in the chaos. *Tommy Kent.*

The bubble of delight evaporated, and suddenly the chill from outside hit her full force. What was she doing, loitering there in his arms as if she thought she should belong? This was exactly the reason she'd brought Janelle. She couldn't trust herself to be levelheaded with Tommy Kent. Where was a girl's best friend when she needed her?

Dre disentangled her rebellious arms, ignoring the twinge of disappointment and not allowing herself to relish in the fact that Tom's hold on her slid away with apparent reluctance— his hands maintaining contact for as long as possible as he stepped back.

Well, not allowing much.

His eyes searched hers, warm, and was there a hint of longing in them?

Of course there was. That was the game he'd perfected in high school. Dre moved backward twos steps, into the safety of her house and the sanity of distance she'd pried between them. That way she could think rationally.

Tom followed her inside, his gaze only shifting from her for a moment while he shut the front door. And then there he was again. Standing deliciously near, attention locked on her, beckoning a physical response as if she were a june bug and he were the electric light of a bug zapper.

"They have one stipulation."

Who did? What was a stipulation again?

"They want to see a design and an outlined plan for how you're going to make it happen."

Design. Plan. Things she should know about. Yep. She could design and plan—she had the gift of vision—and right then, drifting in the tender, smiling gaze he kept on her, she saw all sorts of beautiful things. Things that had virtually nothing to do with a barn and twinkle lights...

Except for maybe a June evening, a white gown, his warm smile, and the start of a future that involved him and her and forever...

What. The. Hay bales? This was not the kind of dream she chased. Visionary, yes. Fool, she tried really hard not to be.

"Dre?"

She shook her head, forced her eyes away from him so that her brain would restart. "Yeah." Design and plan...for the barn. For *Christmas*. That was what was happening right now. The barn she would decorate for Christmas. Not to start a forever with her brother's best friend. Who happened to be a *player*.

Where on earth was Janelle?

"So you can come up with a plan to show the council?"

Her mind shifted enough to reengage. "Yes. Actually, I already have one."

He grinned, and fireworks exploded in her chest. For the love.

"For some reason, I'm not surprised." He stepped forward, sliding a hand to her back, and walked toward the kitchen, where her laptop sat on the table. As if he should be touching her. Escorting her. Making her heart do all the flippy-flop stuff it was doing in that moment.

He tapped the chair in front of her computer. "Show me what you've got."

Why not? He did get her a permit from the city council in record time. She awakened the screen while he stepped into the kitchen, certainly fetching himself a cup of coffee. Because he belonged in this house as much as he did his own and knew his way around.

Something sweet and warmly beautiful settled into her heart in that moment. Even if she was still mad at him for stuff in the past that she probably shouldn't be upset about, here he was, being kind of perfect, belonging in her world, and validating who she was. And getting his own coffee.

As he scooted a chair beside her, close enough to allow her to soak in his body heat, she let her resentment go for the moment. Her design program bloomed onto the screen, and then she was lost in the vision. Showing him what could be and telling him how they could get it done. Full enthusiasm erased any thought of pulling away, holding back, and by the time she finished her impromptu presentation, Tom was entranced.

"They'll love it," he said, focus still on the screen. He'd draped an arm over the chair and was leaning to see the screen.

Dre sat back and turned to look at him. It took a moment for his attention to move to her, but when it did, it locked. She found herself captivated by the tiny flecks of dark brown in his blue eyes. She'd always been a little bit mesmerized by that unusual DNA quirk. His gaze caressed her face, a slow, steady study that had her mentally tumbling right back to where she'd been in the doorway. In his arms.

His hand came off the back of the chair and lifted toward her jawline. When he stalled, his touch hovering, she bit her bottom lip, and the kiss they'd shared years before flooded her mind. It'd been...

Slow. Tender. Beautiful.

Right up until she'd remembered what Abigail had said and how nauseous Dre had felt by the girl's TMI details. How her disappointment in him hurt like a shot to the stomach.

For some reason, that part of the memory didn't slam her gut quite the way it had back then, so when Tommy's fingers traced the loose hair by her ear and then fell away, she was left with a sensation more like disappointment than relief. And a longing she had a hard time convincing herself to lock away.

His Adam's apple bobbed, and the heat of his gaze simmered as he leaned back. "You're really talented, Dre. Mama Rustin says you're doing amazing things down there in Texas."

"She's my mom, so..."

He glanced to her computer screen. "I don't think she's exaggerating."

Following his gaze back to her design, she studied the mock-up of the barn. It was going to happen. Her first solo public project. The vision that filled her with energy and excitement. Tom made it happen.

"Thank you," she whispered, only realizing he might take her gratitude for only the compliment. She glanced at him and then motioned to the computer. "I mean, thank you for this. For getting me this chance. And also, for—" Words tumbled over themselves like a two-year-old testing out stairs for the first time. Heat tinged her cheeks.

Tom smiled. The easy, teasing kind. "I get to help, right?"

She chuckled. "Only if you take direction. This isn't going

to look like your bedroom window at Christmastime."

He laughed. "Mom said hang lights in the window. I did." In a single clump right in the middle of the frame, which faced the road. Every. Single. Year. Anytime anyone would mention Tommy's decorating, his mom would perch her hands on her hips and give him the kind of glare that said she was more amused than irritated.

He kind of had that effect on people. People like Dre. And dang it, if she didn't sort of love that about him.

***

Driving morphed into an unfamiliar and quite possibly unsafe chore as Tom set his truck toward the Rustin ranch. Shifting gears, finding the right turns, remembering to stop at the big red octagonal-shaped signs that said *STOP*. They all felt like clumsy, foreign acts he couldn't focus on, likely making him a danger to himself and others.

Couldn't be helped. His mind was numb.

He could have kissed her. Pretty sure she'd have kissed him back, with the way her eyes warmed and softened, the way those lips parted and her breath stuttered.

Ah. He could have. Wanted to with every electrified pulse that had slugged through him. But he'd done that once and could still feel the sting of that five-year-old slap. See the accusations and disappointment in her hard-as-nails stare. Feel the deep-set chill of her long-enduring silence.

Not things he wanted to repeat. And the guard she'd erected right after their initial reunion two days before, as well as the way she'd made sure Janelle had been always present and between him and her that entire first evening, told him she still had a big old problem with him.

One that he got. One that he deeply regretted.

Kissing her out of sheer desire wasn't going to get them past that. In fact, it'd probably make it worse. She'd remember exactly what she thought of him then—and he'd be pinned by the shame of having behaved like such a boy. Let this whole thing play out that way again, and when she left this time, she'd be gone from his life for good. It'd be his own fault.

If he'd learned anything over the past few years, it'd been that self-control had its virtues. Not that he was good at it, but this was big. Winning her respect back was really important, and it would take more than impulsive acts of chemistry.

But the chemistry. Oh man, the chemistry. Made for some heady, borderline-stupid driving. When his boots landed safely on the frozen dirt driveway at the Rustin ranch, Tom sent a prayer of gratitude up toward heaven. Because, honestly, he couldn't remember half the drive out.

Chapter Seven

Tom had arranged for Dre to meet with the council at four that afternoon.

She perfected her design, double-checked that her outlined plan of action was sound, and agonized over what to wear.

Of all the dumb things to stress about. Her wardrobe? She wasn't the type to make a big deal about her appearance. And yet she spent a ridiculous amount of time focusing on exactly that.

If this was a professional engagement, she'd wear something that reflected professionalism. A suit coat and maybe a pencil skirt that she'd left behind when she'd moved. But it was Mr. Stanton, Mr. Harper, and Mrs. Sampson. They'd all seen her as a freckled-faced, sunburnt kid running around the town park with the pack of boys who were her brother's friends. Had been around the riding arena as she'd learned to sit a trot, and then a lope, on her mare Pal. They'd been in the stands cheering on their own kids when she'd broken her nose playing basketball her freshman year of high school.

Was there any way to appear professional in front of people who had literally watched you grow up?

Plus, she wasn't actually a professional. She was a student. Just a hometown kid with a lot of dreams in her head. And by a lot, they all knew she had more than most, and many of them had been...fanciful at best.

So then, jeans and a nice sweater would be fine. Totally fine.

Either way, Tommy's warm smile would wrap her in a sense of beauty.

Where'd those thoughts come from? Sentiments she wasn't entertaining right now, for the love. Or ever. Which *might* be why she'd focused on the distraction of wardrobe...

At three thirty, she straightened the gray pencil skirt and tugged the sleeves of her velvet suit coat over her arms.

"So, professional it is, huh?" Janelle grinned as she walked back into Dre's bedroom, having witnessed the four outfits Dre had changed into and out of during the previous forty minutes.

"Yes." Dre forced a confident smile that lasted no more than five seconds. "Maybe." She stepped sideways, inspecting her profile in the mirror. "What do you think?"

"Same thing I thought forty minutes ago. You're going to do fine. This is happening. The meeting is a formality because that guy you keep insisting—like a crazy woman—that you don't like, made sure it'd happen. So relax. You've got this."

Dre ignored the reference to Tom. She slipped on her shoes, and refusing to glance at the mirror again lest she decide to try on yet another outfit, she marched toward the door.

Ready or not. She grinned. If that was a choice, she picked ready, and decided that Janelle was right. She could do this. And wouldn't that be a gold star on her résumé—the one that hopefully she'd have the opportunity to show Tami Cooper before the end of the spring semester?

"You girls off?" Mama called from the kitchen.

"Yep, gonna go wow some suits." Dre slipped into her wool dress coat and grabbed her purse.

"You bet." A smile carried in Mama's voice. "And when you get back, let's think about those molasses drop cookies you make, hmm? Picked up a jar of molasses the moment I heard you were coming home."

Janelle's eyebrows lifted with interest. "Cookies too? I keep discovering how much you've been holding out. Why haven't you been cooking for us at school?"

Dre's grin widened, though she waved Janelle's comment off. "You do know that I left the recipe in the box for you, right, Mama? You could make them yourself anytime. Just like the tomato soup."

Mama passed through the doorframe between the kitchen and entry, smiling. "And steal your thunder? I wouldn't dream of it." She winked, reached to pat Dre's cheek, and then gripped her hand. "You go do your thing, bumpkin-girl."

Dre squeezed the hand on hers, nodded, and turned, snatching her laptop as she moved for the door.

Small towns being what they were, it took a full six minutes to walk out the front door and park in front of the city administration building. Dre rolled her shoulders back, pulled open the heavy door, and held it while Janelle passed through. Their shoes made a clicking echo against the marble floor until they stopped by a bench on the far end of the big vaulted room. There sat Paul and Tom, eager grins in place.

"What are you doing here?" Dre addressed Paul because it seemed rude to ask that of Tom. After all, she owed this chance to him. Plus, she couldn't look at Tom. Not without hoping that warm smile she'd forbidden from her thoughts would, in fact, wrap her in beauty.

"Thought we'd come to see you in action," Paul said.

"It's not a show."

Paul's smile fell. "Oh. I didn't mean it like an insult, Dre. I'm sorry."

There it was again. A reminder that her brother had

changed. Didn't want to be a source of frustration and embarrassment to her.

"We don't have to stay." Paul stood, as did Tom.

"No." Dre reached for Paul's elbow. "Sorry. I'm edgy." She swallowed, glanced at Tom. He watched her, and Dre wondered if he was disappointed in her.

The possibility feathered shame across her heart. She had things in there she needed to address.

But not now.

Dre lifted her chin, looked both men in the eyes, and lifted a smile. "I'm glad for the support."

Paul gripped her elbow, and Tom turned, sweeping a hand toward the double doors of the conference room where the meeting was to take place. He waited while she and Paul passed, and then stepped beside Janelle, who walked only a pace behind Dre and Paul.

"You're quite the hero in this," Janelle whispered, not so quietly. "How did you know Dre could pull it all together so quickly?"

Tom chuckled softly. "I know Dre."

"Apparently so."

Dre could feel both sets of eyes on her back, and easily imagined Janelle's knowing smirk. The girl was not doing her job. At all. The traitor.

"Andrea Rustin." Mr. Stanton stood from his place at the head of the heavy wood table. No smile on his face or in his voice.

Dre felt her insides wobble. Paul's grip on her elbow squeezed, a silent encouragement, and Tom flanked her left side, the brush of his palm against her lower back way more thrilling than it ought to be.

She stepped forward, out of the protective fold of her brother and his best friend and on her own before Mr. Stanton and the other two members of the city council. "Mr. Stanton. Thank you for meeting with me on such short notice." She smiled.

"Seems that we must, as this last-minute idea of yours needs immediate approval." Mr. Stanton glanced toward Tom.

Mrs. Sampson stood and reached across the table to shake Dre's hand, cutting off Mr. Stanton with the motion. "Don't buy his bluster, Dre. I can't wait to see what you do with our barn." She motioned to the chair across from her. "Show us what you've got."

Dre ignored the crusty scowl that passed Mr. Stanton's face and focused on Mrs. Sampson as she slid into the chair offered. Paul sat next to Mrs. Sampson on the opposite side of the table, and Janelle dropped onto the chair beside him, leaving Tom to fill the space beside Dre.

He sat back at a distance, as if he wanted her to shine all on her own. Or maybe Dre imagined it.

"It's pretty straightforward." Dre plunged into her presentation as her laptop came to life. And the thrill of possibility carried her through. Her mock-up of the barn, all dressed in holiday cheer, probably could have sold them on her plan by itself. It was pretty spectacular—largely because the old barn was something all on its own. She'd only highlighted its beauty and taken advantage of its central location.

Dre outlined how she envisioned getting it done—with the help of many, and a lighting party/barn dance that would follow. As well as some suggested activities that would follow the barn lighting over the course of time between Thanksgiving and Christmas. Ideas that she wouldn't be around to see through—a fact that carried some disappointment for her because they'd sure be fun.

A chili cook-off. Cheese and wine tasting. And a Christmas piñata, because why not be quirky? It'd be fun. Ideas that would use the historic space as a community builder and would reflect well on the city council. And would justify the time and money spent decorating the barn. If they needed more reasons.

Mrs. Sampson grinned wide. Old Mr. Harper's eyes shone with approval. Mr. Stanton...remained the impassable Mr. Stanton. One eyebrow cocked. "What's in this for you, Ms. Rustin?"

Dre sat back. "Nothing. I guess."

"Nothing?" He pinned her with a doubtful look.

She squirmed. "I guess, the satisfaction of an idea brought to life. And maybe the possibility of our community brought together."

"You won't even be here for most of that. In fact, it seems you've moved on from Rock Creek. Have barely been home since you left for school. Why bother?"

It didn't seem like a bother, so the question hit her as if from nowhere. Dre sat there a little stunned.

"I hear you're studying design," Mr. Stanton pressed. "Is this just an assignment? Something you can add to your résumé—at our cost?"

"No." The word came out defensive. It shouldn't have. But, well, it would be nice to put it on a résumé. Hadn't she thought that earlier? Did that make it selfish? Wrong? Why was Mr. Stanton always looking on the sour side of everything? The year she'd set up a lemonade stand in the very same city park they were currently discussing, the old curmudgeon informed her that she didn't have a permit for soliciting on city property and kicked her budding enterprise right out of the Settler's Park. She'd been all of ten.

He hadn't changed one bit. How on earth did he keep landing in public office?

Mrs. Sampson rolled her eyes and slapped the table near Mr. Stanton. "Charles, you're such a Scrooge. And even if it is an assignment or a boon on her résumé, who cares? It's a great plan, and it wouldn't hurt you to admit it." She turned to look at Dre again. "I say yes. An emphatic yes to the lights, and we will absolutely be considering the other ideas. And also, don't let the old grump get to you."

She was a refreshing addition to the council. How long ago had she been voted in?

Mr. Harper muffled a chuckle. "I vote yes as well. And have no problem appointing a budget for the lights and the added electrical costs. It'll be worth it, and we always have money to spare in the budget because someone among us seems to think that money is *only* for squirreling away."

That someone didn't need to be named, but he was also an enigma of sorts. His family lived in obvious wealth. His son, Chuck—who was Paul and Tom's age—loved to flaunt that fact. But Charles Stanton Senior? He was a miser, especially when it came to spending money on the town.

But it seemed, on this occasion, he was outvoted. That was not to be had, so he nodded his approval, the three came to an agreement on funding, and then they dismissed the last-minute gathering.

It was happening. Standing in the foyer with Janelle, Paul, and Tom, Dre bit the corner of her bottom lip as a smile spread over her face. Tom met her eyes, a smile on his face. And yes, the warmth there made her feel beautiful.

She was too happy in that moment to try to swat it away.

***

The four of them met at Allen's Hardware Store, energy buzzing between them like they were a pack of high schoolers about to pull a prank. Dre brushed that image aside, because Paul had pulled enough not-so-harmless pranks that had landed him in lots of trouble.

This wasn't a prank.

Tom rubbed his hands together as he approached the sales counter where Erin Moore waited behind the register.

"Well, Tommy Kent." Erin smiled. "Didn't imagine you'd

be hanging around town over Thanksgiving."

"Yep," Tom said. "We need lights. Lots and lots of lights."

"Lights?" Erin lifted her eyebrows. "What kind of lights?"

"Twinkly lights." Dre stepped forward. "On strands—preferably the dark-green strands, not white. But the lights should be white, not yellow. Or they could be yellow, as long as they're all yellow. Not mixed—the white and yellow. The lightbulbs all need to be the same."

Erin stared at Dre like she was nuts. "Uh. Okay. So Christmas lights?"

"Right."

"Okay. Do you know how much?"

Dre nodded, reached in her purse for the little notepad on which she'd written out a supply list, and handed over the number she'd calculated for linear footage of twinkly lights. Erin glanced at the number, eyebrows shooting toward her hairline, and then looked back up at Dre. "You've got to be kidding."

Tom squeezed Dre's shoulder and spoke to Erin. "You've got them, right?"

"Do you know how many strands of lights this would be? You could cover the entire roof of a house with this. You're not attempting a Clark Griswold here, are you?"

Paul laughed. "That would be fun. What do you think, Tom? We could get enough to do your house."

"Don't even think about it." Dre rolled her eyes at her brother. "He'd hang them up in clumps and call it good."

"Hey, come on now." Tom nudged her side. "Allow that a guy could grow up a little bit."

"Right." Dre smirked, then turned back to Erin. "We're not trying to replicate *Christmas Vacation*, I promise. We're decorating the barn in Settler's Park. On Friday—you're welcome to come."

Erin seemed to consider the idea for a minute, then nodded.

"That old barn would look fantastic all lit up. I love it."

"Thanks." Dre grinned. "So, lights. Can you help us out? Also, we'll need these other supplies." She handed the page containing her written list over the counter. Erin looked it over, nodded, and then moved around the counter toward the electrical aisle. "Most of what you'll need is down here. I'll go to the back room to see how many rolls of lights we've got. Hopefully, enough—and oh boy, Dad's head is going to explode when he finds out he's been wiped clean on Christmas lights right before Thanksgiving."

"Oh." Dre stopped midstride. "Is this going to hurt your business?"

Erin smiled. Shook her head. "Nah. We should be able to get a quick order in tonight and have it in-house by Friday morning. He'll flip out because this is unexpected, is all. He's all about the projections. Planning."

"Ah," Dre said.

Paul patted her shoulder. "A kindred spirit, right, Dre?"

"Nothing wrong with having a plan."

"Right." Erin nodded, swiped a stack of baskets off the floor by the door, and handed them to the group. "If you want to start on the other supplies, I'll see what I can find out back. We'll have you ready in no time."

True to her word, Erin found what she could and had the boxes out front within minutes. Checking out, however, took some doing, and it was a good thing Tom and Paul had driven Tom's pickup, because there was no way it would all fit into Dre's little Camry. After a stop at the barn to drop off and store their loot, the group met at Ms. May's for coffee and pie.

A Rock Creek tradition Dre had keenly missed. Even if she wasn't saying it out loud.

"You know that you owe me now, right, sis?" His flannel sleeves rolled to his elbows, Paul leaned his arms on the table.

"What?"

"Fair's fair. I need help down on the river property Wednesday. Sorting. Loading. Giving a few vaccinations—which, if memory serves right, you're the best in the family with that one. So. Hope you didn't leave your cowgirl-up down in Texas."

Dre actually loved a day working cattle, so Paul's backhanded request wasn't asking much—except Janelle would freak. Her friend sounded down home with her sweet Texan drawl, and she wore the cowboy boots to match the talk. But Janelle had grown up in Houston and had an irrational but stubborn fear of household pets. Roundup wasn't going to float her boat. Unless it was to an ER somewhere to treat a sudden onset of PTSD.

Dre sat back, crossed her arms. "Whoa there, boy. What is it you think I owe you for?"

"The barn, of course." Paul grinned. "One phone call and it's done."

"*Tom* made the phone call. And I made the plan."

"And who called Tom?"

Dre's look slid from her brother to Tom, who held his mug in one hand and sported half a grin, amusement lighting his eyes.

"Can you believe this?" Dre shook her head. "Just like high school, when he'd find the smart kids to pair up with and take all the credit for their hard work."

"He's *your* brother." Tom chuckled and shrugged. "Although, he might have a point. Fair is fair."

Dre smacked the table. "What?"

"I'm working down there too, and the extra help would be welcome. So..."

Janelle laughed. The snort-giggle kind Dre knew. It meant *he's flirting, and it's so cute.*

He might have been flirting. And, for the love, cute. Dang it. Dre forced a frown, bundling up the giddy girl who threatened to betray her and stuffing her into the basement of her heart. "Is this a conspiracy?"

Tom thunked his mug on the table as he leaned against the edge. "Come on, Dre. You love to ride, and I know pushing cattle around happens to be one of your specialties. Don't try to tell me you haven't missed the ranch work. And the river property? You love it there."

Paul smacked Tom's back. "Best place on earth."

Dre caught Janelle's look from the corner of her eye. The one that asked, *How does he know these things about you?*

"Best place on earth, huh?" Janelle nudged Dre's arm. "You didn't tell me you had one of those in Nebraska too."

"Everyone has their own."

"Guess so." Janelle winked. "Are you gonna show me?"

"You're going to work cattle?"

"Ha!" Janelle shook her head. "Not on your life."

"Can't spend all day in the truck."

"Sure I could. I have an iPad. My cell phone. A loaded music app. Leave me a couple of bottles of water—and some of that soup you've been hiding from me. I could be set for days."

Paul shook his head. "That wouldn't be any fun at all. Aren't you from Texas?"

"Houston, cowboy." Janelle raised an eyebrow.

One corner of Paul's mouth lifted. "Thought they were from Dallas."

Dre snorted. "I see what you did there."

Paul grinned as if he were brilliant.

Tom cleared his throat. "Okay, enough of the fun and games. Let's talk serious business here. Are you going or not?" He settled those steel blues on her, more hope in them than probably he realized. In a moment, Dre's mind went back to yesterday afternoon. To his zeroed-in and locked-down gaze full of warmth. And oh, the feel of his thumb running an electric current down her neck with the anticipation of his touch.

For the love. What was wrong with her? A full day of working cattle might do her some good. Smells of horse, cattle, working pens, and sweat. Sore muscles from riding, pushing, sorting, and loading. Set her mind straight.

Yeah. A full day working pens with Tom would totally do that.

Dre breached the gaze lock Tom had pulled her into and shook her head. "I don't know, boys. Janelle has a major project due when we get back, and I've got a presentation I have to finish."

"You finished it," Janelle said.

Because she was a snitch. Should have left her in Texas.

"However, she's right about me. I'm kind of buried with this research report I've got due. All the more reason for Dre to go though. I'll be no fun at all, stuck in the books."

Paul grinned, his eyes bouncing from Dre to Tom.

What was that about?

"It's settled then." Paul stood, flipped his wallet out of his back pocket, and tossed some money onto the table. "Time my sister remembered where she came from. Supposed to snow on Wednesday." He winked as Tom stood up beside him. "Dress warm. Should be fun."

Three against one? When did Paul get in on this? What was *this*, anyway?

Chapter Eight

"I don't think you're really taking your purpose here seriously." Dre crossed her arms as she leaned against her dresser, scowl pinned on Janelle.

From her sprawled-out-on-her-stomach position on the bed, Janelle quirked an eyebrow. "I'm seriously doubting your sanity. Go. I've got this project to work on, and a whole potful of soup. And after that, snuggling up with a good book in a quiet house that lacks the homey sounds of constant quarrelling with a hefty dash of angry shouts sounds like a dream holiday to me. So go. Work cattle. Be all cowgirlish. And for heaven's sake, *flirt*."

Dre jabbed a finger Janelle's direction. "Stop right there."

"Ever hear the phrase *hungry eyes*?"

"He does *not* have hungry eyes."

Janelle lifted her brows. "I wasn't talking about him."

"What?" Heat filled Dre's face. She smacked her palms over her certain-to-be-red cheeks and groaned. "That's our problem. I told you—"

"Nope. Not gonna do it, Dre. I'm straight-up dumb-whipped by your stubbornness, and I most certainly am not going to stand in Tom Kent's way when he's clearly more than you've given him credit for. Not to mention completely wrapped up with you. And also, *you like him*."

"That was never the issue." Dre covered the threat of delight at Janelle's claim about Tom with an exasperated huff. "He's a—"

"Player?" Janelle held up a hand and sat up. "Yeah. Heard that one. Not seeing it, girlfriend. Maybe what you think you know isn't the whole story. Or maybe he's grown up. Changed. Maybe you're hanging on to some old hurts and disappointments because you think you're safer that way. In any case, I think you're cutting off some pretty amazing opportunities, and I'm not going to help you with that. I've seen enough dysfunctional and cyclical resentment in my own family to know that's not what I want for my best friend. It's no way to live, Dre."

The past two days had been dizzying enough. Now Dre's head spun with Janelle's bold stand against her. Janelle wasn't wrong about letting go of some old hurts. But this whole week was going down exactly the wrong path. Dre hadn't come home expecting to deal with *her* issues.

She'd come back to Rock Creek with a plan. Spend some long-overdue quiet time with her mama and daddy and her aging grandparents. Check up on Paul because it was the sisterly thing to do. And then get the heck back where her plans were clear and optimized, her life unmuddied, and far, far away from the two young men who'd wrapped her up in knots.

She backtracked to the *check on Paul* part of the plan, because the passing thought had snarled on a bit of guilt. Not liking the tug and consequential burn, she took a good, hard heart check. She'd expected to find Paul still his old disastrous self. More alarming, buried deep within her was an unsettling emotion to discover that wasn't true.

Paul had changed. Everything about him now was anything but selfish chaos. He was stable, kind, responsible, respectful, and maybe most significantly, repentant. His apology had rocked Dre every bit as much as it had soothed. Why was that?

Whatever the reason, Dre knew it was wrong. That it revealed an ugliness within her heart she hadn't been aware of. And that, in a strange circular sort of way, brought her back to Tommy Kent. Because Janelle had nailed it.

Tom was still the boy Dre had crushed on as an early teenager. But he was not the young man Dre had been crushed by later in high school.

She'd kept alive the disappointments and hurts as if they were a shield keeping her heart safe. Her pristine plans in place. Even though the evidence in front of her declared both Paul and Tom to be different now than they'd been, she didn't want to accept it.

What did that say about her?

The burn in her gut flared.

People changed—especially when God moved and they let Him work. She'd thought she'd believed that. Clearly, though, she didn't. Not in her core—where it mattered—with the people she cared about, had been hurt by, and was determined to keep safely out.

She should be rejoicing about the men God was shaping. Instead, she was holding on to fear with both fists.

And Janelle was calling her out on it.

"Say yes, or you'll force my hand." Janelle pushed up on her knees, bouncing on the mattress.

Dre couldn't hold back a chuckle. "What does that mean?"

"I'll go." She crossed her arms, cocked her head. "And flirt."

"With my brother? Mom said he's dating Haylee—a girl he's dated on and off since high school—so good luck there."

An ornery smirk pressed on Janelle's mouth, and she shook her head.

With Tom? Dre's heart clenched.

"Would that just do it?" Janelle said, her wide smile growing.

Dre grabbed a pair of clean socks rolled together and tossed them at her. Janelle fell back against the pillows in a fit of laughter. "She's got..." She lifted a fist to her mouth as if she were holding a mic and sang a slightly altered version of the hit from *Dirty Dancing*.

Dre launched at her, tackling the smaller, willowy young woman in a fit of embarrassed laughter. If anything, Janelle knew how to make an awkward moment bearable. Laughable, even. Who couldn't love that in a friend?

Later, when Janelle's music-less karaoke ended and the house was settled and quiet, Dre lay beneath her thick quilt trying not think about blue eyes flecked with brown, and lyrics about magic and feelings that wouldn't subside.

Lyrics that were proving a little more true to her life than she'd planned.

She should have outgrown this crush by now. He was her older brother's best friend. Little sisters were supposed to quit that scenario when they left home and got their own lives. Why hadn't she? Tommy had been the boy out of reach— always around and usually nice, but not for her. Because she was Paul's little sister, and how weird would that be?

Would it still be weird, now that they were grown up?

She let the five-year-old memory slide in. The one where he'd cupped her face. Watched her eyes while he lowered his head, as if to make sure she knew he saw *her*. And then...

A shiver rippled down her spine as she relived that moment.

"I wouldn't really do it, you know." Janelle's whisper came from the cot on the other side of the room. The one Janelle had insisted she'd use, because Dre hadn't been home in so long, she should obviously get to sleep in her old bed. The girl was fantastically stubborn. And thoughtful.

"What?"

"Flirt with Tom. I wouldn't do that to you."

Dre didn't know what to say. Nor could she explain the rush of relief.

Hungry eyes? Questionable. Her heart though?

She shut her eyes, willing sleep to snatch away the tumbling thoughts. Tom's kiss found her again. Right there where it didn't belong in her dreams.

***

"I've got a real question." Paul tossed Tom's saddle onto the saddle tree in the trailer's tack room and turned to grab the bridle and reins Tom held out to him.

Tom inhaled. "As opposed to a fake one?" He'd wondered when Paul was gonna ask. Waited the whole blustery day as they worked on Paul's grandparents' land for him to bring it up. Wondered why he'd waited until almost sundown while they loaded stuff up for the trip to the river property in the morning.

Better Paul ask now than tomorrow, though. Tom wouldn't put that past his friend—asking in front of Dre just to make them both squirm.

Paul took the leather straps from Tom but didn't hang them on the rack. "One hundred percent serious here, Tom. No kidding. No jabbing."

"Why'd I stay for Thanksgiving?"

"No, I'm not an idiot. I already know that answer. How long have you loved her?"

Love...that might be pushing it a bit. Hadn't seen Dre in quite a while. And last time he had, they'd basically been kids. For the most part. Kids who'd lip-locked. Could a man call that love?

Did he love her? Obsessed might be the better term for the moment, because he sure couldn't get Dre Rustin out of his head. Not for anything, and that'd been a problem for quite a while. Since they were those kids who'd lip-locked.

No. Before that. He'd kissed her then for the same reason

he'd stayed in Rock Creek for the holiday. Couldn't stop thinking about her. Worrying about her. Wishing he could fix things for her when it came to Paul.

"Tom?"

Tom raised his eyes to meet Paul's, who stood above him on the trailer, arms now crossed and waiting for an answer.

"I don't know. Can't say for sure it's love."

An eyebrow pushed toward Paul's hat line. "You can't? Have you seen your face when you look at her?"

"Is *that* a real question?"

Paul chuckled. "How long though?"

"Long time."

"Why didn't you say anything?"

"Back in our school days, that would have been a disaster. Do you remember your obnoxious self back then?"

Paul rubbed his neck. "Yeah."

A spark of guilt flickered in Tom's chest. He hadn't meant to pick at regrets.

"That far back, huh?" Paul lifted his gaze to meet Tom's again, apparently not bothered too much by the reminder of where he'd been.

"I don't know. I remember worrying about her. Thinking that she was juggling a lot trying to keep you away from trouble—and sometimes death—and out of your dad's range of frustration. It wore on her, you know?"

"Yeah. I do know."

"So I looked out for her, was all. Mostly. And—" Tom stemmed his words. Why was he telling Paul this?

"And?"

Because Paul was his best friend. More importantly, Paul was Dre's older brother.

"I kissed her. Once."

"You did what?"

Tom met Paul's mild challenge with an unflinching stare.

Because, no, he wasn't ashamed of that kiss. There were things he was ashamed of—things that didn't directly involve Dre. But kissing her? Not one of them.

Paul nodded. "When?"

"You're nosey."

"She's my sister."

"You know I'd never hurt her."

"That's true. But I have an older brother obligation. You'd understand if you had a sister."

"That night out at Harper's Pond. When I pulled you out of the fight with Chuck and took you home while you were still bloody and wasted. I went back to check on Dre, because I knew she was going to be devastated."

Paul looked toward his boots, hand rubbing his neck again, and nodded. "Because that was it. Dad sent me to Omaha after that." He peeked at Tom, hung up the bridle set, and shoved his hands into his pockets.

Neither spoke as Tom handed him the next saddle and blanket—Dre's. Paul finished loading the tack they'd need for the day's work down at the river property, shut the door and made sure the handle latched, and then turned back to Tom.

"Long time then."

Tom settled his hands in his Carhartt coat pockets and nodded.

"But you're not gonna call it love?"

He shrugged. "Don't know."

"Does she know? That you've missed her, I mean. Did you tell her?"

"She's...cautious about me. So, no."

A grin broke Paul's serious expression—the first since this conversation began. "It starts with a date, you know."

Tom rolled his eyes and shoved Paul's shoulder. Like the guy actually knew what it was like. Paul's longest relationship was with Haylee, a long-running episode of three months on, six months off, two months on, nine months off...

Like that was going anywhere. Paul had no clue what it was like to be in love.

Then again, Tom wasn't calling it love, was he?

Chapter Nine

Holy frostbite. November really decided to be cold.

Of course it would on the day they were heading down to the river property to work outside all day with the cows.

Dre cupped her travel mug full of hot coffee with both mitted hands and snuggled into the fleece gator covering her neck and chin while she waited for Tom to open the back door to Paul's pickup.

"Your nose is red already." Tom tucked a hand under her elbow as she climbed into the backseat of the king cab.

He smacked the door shut and hopped into the front, where he'd been when the guys stopped to pick her up. Buckled in, Paul eased out onto the road in the dark. Her, the boys, and the horses, off to work in the freezing cold.

"I know, and I've only been outside for three minutes." She grinned, though Tom probably didn't see it because she'd nudged the gray gator up over her nose, and it was before daybreak. "Should be a fun day."

Though she'd slathered her voice with sarcasm, she doubted that either one of the men in the front of the pickup took her seriously. They knew her deep love of the place. If it weren't so far away from the mite bit of civilization the little town of Rock Creek provided, she was certain Grams and Pop would be living in the little crackerbox house that overlooked the oxbow pond of the river property.

"Should warm up when the sun lights the sky," Paul said.

Tom chuckled softly. "Yeah, until those snow clouds out west make their way overtop of us."

"Snow on the river property." Paul shot a quick glance over his shoulder. "Still love that, don't you, Dre?"

His attention didn't stay on her, because driving and all. Didn't matter. He didn't need an answer—they all knew without her saying. If there was something she missed about Rock Creek, it was working outside—especially on her grandparents' river property.

Well, she missed more than that. Pie and coffee at Ms. May's. Mama's warm hand on her cheek as she called her *bumpkin-girl*. The way Daddy's mouth would flicker a bit of a proud smile when they shared an exclusive glance. Paul's ornery streak—when kept in the mild range.

Tom Kent.

For the love. She sighed into the fleece still swaddling her face.

Okay, fine. It didn't change anything to admit it, did it? She missed him. Missed the way he'd chuckle quietly when Paul would belt out a belly laugh at whatever the two of them had found funny. Missed the way he'd taken to defending her to Paul in their last few years of high school—especially when Paul was critical about however she'd handled his latest episode of self-destruction. Missed the way she'd felt when Tom's gaze had landed on her. Only her. Especially that one time...

And that was where the admission could turn toxic. And the reason she'd brought Janelle to Nebraska in the first place. Why the heck had she left her best friend asleep in her warm, cozy room this morning?

"Warming up yet?" Hooking an elbow over the seat, Tom turned to face her.

She met his eyes, and even in the pre-sunrise darkness where she could barely see, a warm, gooey sensation puddled in her chest. It drained down to her toes when he bowed a finger over the gator and pushed it down, brushing her nose and top lip with the motion.

"That hot coffee should help." He nodded to her mug, and the gravel of his morning voice finished the melting.

Didn't need it, because, yep. She was definitely warm now.

Holy hay bales, she was pathetic. She reached to set her travel mug in the cup holder, forcing him to move his hand out of her space. Because clearly she couldn't handle any sort of proximity. At all.

"I'm gonna save the warmth for when I need it." *Because you melted the chill right out of me...* Oh goodness, she was *so* pathetic. For. The. Love. Her cheeks felt like she'd been pulled out of a 350-degree oven, and she was certain they looked like cherry Jell-O. "What I mean is, I'm going to sleep. For now. Until we get there. So coffee is a bad idea. Because coffee and sleeping don't mix. And also, I might spill. If I drift off..."

Stop talking!

Warm amusement played over Tom's mouth. Paul glanced back again, his eyebrows squished up in the *you're nuts* position. Dre reached for the edge of the gator and tugged it back over her nose, wishing it wouldn't be totally weird for her to position it over her face.

Tom shifted, pushing a shoulder into the seat. "Is this your normal before-sun-up self? Or is it caffeine depravation at work here?"

"Both. Probably." She cleared her throat. Flipped the hood of her sweatshirt over her head and leaned back against the seat.

If she shut her eyes, he'd stop looking at her. Right?

She didn't peek to find out.

***

Two hours and a hefty dose of warm caffeine later, Dre sat in her old leather saddle, the new morning light colliding with the billow of promised snow in the west. It'd taken a good ten minutes to acclimate to the frigid air, and even so, she huddled into her coat and gator, thankful for wool boot socks and insulated gloves.

She settled into the rhythm of her horse's long stride as she and Tom headed their mounts northwest. Oranges, pinks, and gradient hues of blue painted the eastern sky beautiful, and the rolling hills of the grass prairie—though brown this time of year—sang to her a familiar and comforting lullaby.

It felt like going home. Even if the hint of a twinge in her legs and backside warned her that this homecoming might leave her unaccustomed-to-the-saddle muscles sore by the end of the day. This moment. This view. This feeling. It'd be worth it.

"Missed it, huh?" Tom sat tall and easy, heels dropped so his legs looked particularly long, left hand on the reins, right hand resting on his thigh. His mouth curved pleasantly, gaze warm on her.

"You can tell?"

"Tension rolled off your shoulders like steam from the pond."

"Didn't even know I was tense."

One eyebrow jumped. "I seem to have that effect on you."

What to say to that? Dre found nothing, so she scanned the building sunrise in the east and let it roll. Then changed the subject. "Did you know Paul would be taking on a manager for this part of the ranch?"

"Yeah, he's been talking about it. He's utilized the river property more and more over the past couple of years—partly because he's been working on building up his own herd. Partly because he loves it down here and any excuse to make the trip is a good one. But since he's done that, he's spread a little thin. At one point, he talked about moving here—started fixing up the old house to make it livable again. But your grandpa's getting older, so..."

"Mama mentioned Pop wasn't always good these days."

"Yeah. Sometimes he's confused. A couple times, he slept in."

Dre connected with Tom's gaze, alarm seeping into her swaddled warmth. Pop had worked the land and cows his whole eighty-some years of life. Was pure cowboy to the bone. The man didn't know what sleeping in was. Wasn't his way.

"Paul's worried about them," Dre said more than asked.

Tom shrugged. "He looks after them now."

The stinging alarm settled, gave way to a fresh wave of appreciation. She'd missed a lot apparently. But a new swell of pride washed over the tender wounds she'd nursed over the last four years where her brother was concerned. This new man Paul was becoming, he was worth another chance.

And the man riding beside her?

She looked over at Tom. He faced forward, eyes scanning the pasture ahead of them, leaving her with a profile view. It was familiar—still the Tommy Kent she'd known her whole life. Except the boy was gone, leaving only man. One who seemed familiar, yet not the same. The boy she'd known. This man beside her? Maybe she didn't.

Maybe she should.

"Why didn't Paul offer the management position to you?" she asked.

An easy smile moved his face. "He did." He tugged his horse to a stop, dismounted, and opened the north pasture gate with a tug and pull of post and wire that he made look way easier than she knew from experience it actually was.

Dre nudged her mount forward, snatching the reins Tom had left looped on his saddle, and ponied his ride through the gate. She waited until he had the gate latched and was remounted before she pushed the conversation.

"You said no?"

He chuckled. "Don't get me wrong, Dre. Your brother's a pretty good man these days. But working for him the rest of my life wasn't really my plan."

"But you're still in Rock Creek, even though your parents and brother moved to the farm down in Kansas."

"Was there a question in there?"

She met his teasing eyes, lifting her brows.

"You know I went to college, right?" he asked.

Well, yeah. She kind of knew that. Hadn't really thought about it. In her mind, Tom was the same guy she'd worked really hard to ignore. But anyway. What'd college have to do with it? Rock Creek wasn't exactly bursting with opportunities.

"It's home." Tom filled in the pause. "And my degree is in land management—emphasis in soil and water conservation. I liked my studies, and I'd really like to be able to put to use what I learned. All of this"—he swept his hand over the land that rolled before him—"this is lifeblood to me. I love this area. The unique life we live in this unknown pocket of the world. This view. This legacy that we have in our backyards. I want to be able to help preserve what we have—both the lifestyle and the section of earth and wildlife we're allowed to roam—in a way that honors both."

Dre sat a little stunned as the passion Tom clearly felt rang true and clear in the crisp morning air. Conviction and grace twined together in his voice, and as she listened to him, a bulge of yearning pushed within her to see him do what he clearly longed to do.

"Sounds like you've found your calling."

"Part of it."

"But in Rock Creek?"

Again, that chuckle rolled from his chest. The soft rumble was quickly becoming something of an addiction for her ears. Like the distant drumming of a late-summer thunderstorm. Not the violent kind, but the kind that promised a good gentle soaking, along with the fresh smell of their world renewed. The kind that made her smile. And want to stay, to steep in the rain.

"Remember Trace Whitney?" Tom asked.

"From school? Yeah, he was in your class."

"His dad, Jim, has been with the regional Department of Natural Resources for a long time. I did my internship with him. He's going to retire in the next year or so."

"Ah. So you'll have a job. One you want."

A gathering of cattle peppered the next gully as they came over the small rise. Their loot. Should be an easy drive back to the working pens Paul and his potential new manager were setting up. They'd have a couple more pastures to ride, and then the dirty work would begin. But for now, it was just her and Tom.

Maybe they could take the drive slow.

"Hope so." He reined his horse around, and the animal did an impatient little dance—because she was a cow pony, and she was ready to work. Tom grinned. "You thought I was leeching off your grandparents and brother, didn't you?"

"Not even once," she said. Dead serious, because the thought had never entered her mind.

"I *can* cowboy. In case you thought I was a charity case for your brother."

"I never doubted. I've seen you on a horse."

"Not lately." A dare glinted in his eyes while his horse continued to sidestep, anxious to get to it. "And actually, it's been a while since you've been in a saddle. Let's see if you can still stay on."

She glanced at the herd and back to him. With a smirk that was very much the boy she remembered, he tugged his pony into a roll back and they were off.

Which was, in fact, a dare. Not one she'd back down from. Even if her backside was going to ache by sundown.

So much for a slow drive. Ah well. It'd be fun just the same.

***

Yeah. She could still ride.

This little setup Paul had arranged was turning into sweet torture, because not only could Dre still cowgirl like she had when she was seventeen, but her smile, sass—now punctuated with an adorable hint of Texas-speak—and determination corralled his heart, undoing about every inch of dignified, manly self-control he had. He saw groveling in his near future.

She'd never get out of his head now.

Chapter Ten

Snow began drifting in giant, feathery flakes right before lunch break—which consisted of cold roast beef sandwiches, carrot sticks, and lukewarm hot cocoa.

The cattle-pushing quartet gathered around Paul's king cab Ford and ate while the clouds drifted as fluffy snow to the ground, quickly melting into the already semi-damp earth.

So it would be mud work for them in the afternoon. At least it'd warmed up a bit. A balmy thirty-ish degrees. Warm enough that Dre had shed her coat, hat, and neck gator and worked in her oversized hoodie and purple Carhartt coveralls. She'd corralled her certain-to-be hat hair in a messy braid and jammed a gray fleece headband over it to keep the stray wisps out of her face.

And Janelle missed all this. Dre grinned into her tin mug as she thought about the worry fit her fashion-forward, always-camera-ready friend would have had if she were here. Nope. This cow-working life wouldn't suit. And that was A-OK. Neither young woman felt like the other had to be or do the same things to justify their choices and lifestyles. A rare gem of friendship there.

"What's that secret little grin for?" Tom moseyed closer, his own tin cup close to his lips.

Dre shrugged, but her mouth stretched into a full smile.

Working with Tom had been fun. He was a version of the old boy she'd known—before he'd decided to be mister lady's-man-with-a-not-so-good reputation. He'd asked her about Texas—what she liked there. About her schooling and what had drawn her to design. Even about her hopes for life beyond school. Every answer she gave—about the Texas sunshine, the wild bluebells and live oaks, the friends she'd made there, chief of which was Janelle, and the way design allowed her to dream with purpose—Tom had nodded, interest in his eyes and his mouth set in the kind of easy grin that captivated her way too often.

He made her feel...important. He made her dreams feel...attainable. He made her long for more of those smiles.

And.

There was definitely an *and* there. And if the man kept pinning that attention that continued to put the *and* in the space between them, she wasn't sure she could keep ignoring it.

"Dre?"

"Yeah." She whipped her gaze up to his as heat surged onto her face. Stupid *and.*

"You okay?"

"Yeah. Of course. You?" She swallowed, trying to bottle up the words. But they were not to be bottled. "I mean, of course you're okay. Standing right there. Just, right there. So we're okay. Right?"

For the love, Dre! Shut. Up!

"I hope we're good." He winked.

Her heart pooled into that big ol' *and* that tickled in her stomach. Had Paul not been standing on the other side of the pickup, she might have reached out to fist a handful of that plaid flannel button-down he was wearing and tasted that *and* curving on his mesmerizing mouth.

She done lost her mind. That was what happened there. She'd taken a backroad trail to crazy and kind of liked it a little too much. Which would explain why she was still entertaining crazy thoughts when Paul walked around the pickup, ducking under the gooseneck of the horse trailer, with his manager-on-trial following his muddy boot tracks.

"So we're going to head down to the highway to make sure the cattle truck will still be able to make it up the drive and down this road in the mud. Tom, you and Dre can handle vaccinating the off-season calves, right?"

"Shouldn't be a problem." Tom set his cup on the edge of the pickup bed and talked to Paul as if everything in the world was completely normal. "You want them turned out when they're done, or are you moving them too?"

Dre tried to find the normal place in the world that used to be familiar. It was a struggle. "Why wouldn't you move them up to Pop's place?"

Looky there. Normal. She did normal—well, faked it really well. Even with the crazy part of her brain still buzzing about crazy things in the background of her mind.

"The off-season calves are mine. Pop's and I thought it'd be cleaner between the two of us to keep them separate." Paul gestured to the man on his right. "Thus, a manager for the river property."

Ah. The picture was coming together. Paul was serious about this ranching thing, which was kind of a one-eighty from the brother she'd run from. That Paul had wanted nothing to do with Rock Creek, let alone Pop's ranch. He'd had "bigger" plans than pushing cows.

Things changed.

Dre's attention snuck back to Tom's profile. Yeah. Things did indeed change. Or maybe they didn't. Maybe she was still that seventeen-year-old girl with a big ol' crush.

"So you'll be good, right?" Paul looked straight at her.

Another wave of heat filled her face. Good? Of course she'd be good. She wouldn't act on any of those crazy *and* ideas with Tom. How'd Paul even know about those anyway?

Oh. Yeah. Good with the vaccinating-the-calves thing.

"Yep. We're good."

Paul chuckled, walked forward, and mussed her hair as he passed. As if he *did* know.

As if.

Dre pushed her shoulders back, set her mug in the bed of the pickup, and grabbed her gloves from the pockets of her coveralls. Paul knew nothing. And that would remain. Because there was nothing to know.

***

Twenty head. Pretty decent year for Paul, building on a start he had for his own herd. Tom mentally congratulated his buddy and gripped the sense of satisfaction and pride to see his best friend's life iron out. For a while, it had looked like it wouldn't.

Not that Tom really had much room to talk. He'd just kept his rebellion a little quieter.

"That one isn't looking so good." Dre nodded at a calf curled up by itself near the far rail.

"No, it doesn't," Tom said. "Might have to load it up with your Pop's cows and have Doc Hansen take a look."

Dre moved for the coiled lasso at the far end of the working pen, her loose braid swishing with her cowgirl stride, and mud caking the bottoms of her overalls all the way to her knees. Man, she was some kind of beautiful mess today. And he'd caught a few looks from her that sewed longing and regret in a tight seam that made breathing a little bit of a challenge.

Apparently quiet rebellion was as messy as full-blown, throw-it-in-your-face rebellion, because he knew exactly why Dre had slapped him five years back, and he was pretty sure she still held all those true-ish rumors against him. Even if, throughout their day of work, she had given him a few doe-eyed looks that ended somewhere in the region of his mouth.

A beautiful mess. That about summed it up. This unspoken thing between him and Dre, the one he was becoming fairly certain she was feeling too. Or fighting against.

Tom swiped the thoughts, and the subsequent gut clench, to the side. They were working calves in a muddy pen, for heaven's sake. Not at all a setup for romance on any level.

"You want me to get him?" he asked.

With a side glance, she eyed him as if he'd insulted her. "I wasn't a rodeo star, but I can get a loop around a calf's head when he's sitting there like he's half-dead. Thank you very much."

He chuckled, and she did exactly that. The Black Angus grunted a pathetic little bawl when she slipped the rope around him, and looked up at her as if he was looking for his mama.

"Huh." Dre touched the animal's ears, then nose, then felt his neck, where she'd easily pick up his pulse. "Maybe he was just napping. So weird. You want to bring me the vacs kit? I'll just—"

...take care of it while he's being nice. That was probably what she was going to say. Except that little three-hundred-plus-pound bugger jumped to his feet and took off.

Dre snatched the rope with her gloved hand as the calf bolted. "The gate!"

Oh, right. The gate was open, because they were turning out the calves when they were done, and the little not-sick one had been their last patient. Tom jumped into action, lunging across the greasy mud to shut the gate.

Dre hung on while the calf ran, dragging her while the animal yelled outrage into the cold, snowy air. The calf had much better footing than Tom, and as they met near the gate—which was the muddiest part of the pen—Tom realized he'd not get it shut in time. Still, the animal bolted, pulling Dre on her stomach through the muck.

"Tom, the gate!" Dre rolled and sputtered, looking more like a mud skier than a cowgirl.

What could he do, besides try hard not to laugh? He lunged for the rope, mud and momentum pushing him to the ground. The calf belted out another round of outrage as the force of Tom's weight jerked him to a stop.

That was how it ended. Dre sprawled out, facedown in the mud. Tom right beside her on his side, now covered in a fresh layer of cold muck. And the calf, as if realizing that he'd woken from a bad dream, turned to them both and lowered his head. All calm and not running. One long bleat, and it stepped toward them like it was apologizing.

The little bugger.

"For the love," Dre muttered, pushing up onto her elbows, both hands still on the rope.

He couldn't hold it in anymore. Laughter bubbled from Tom's belly, and as he rolled to his back, his shoulders shook.

Dre's light-blue eyes flicked from him and then back to the calf. "There is nothing wrong with that steer."

"Nope." Tom breathed out the word between laughs. He flicked off the glove covering his left hand and reached toward her face. "You've got a mud streak from your chin to your ear."

She faced him, and he used his thumb to rub at the brown on her face.

"It's probably not just mud." A hint of a smile cracked on her pretty mouth.

Tom belted out a fresh laugh, and Dre let her own amusement loose. She leaned her head down against his shoulder as a fit of giggles overtook her. When she looked up, she braced a palm against his chest, and her gaze connected with his.

Laughter fizzled.

He held his breath while she studied him, her wide smile fading. He braced himself, expecting her to push against him, leap to her feet, and ignore the heat he saw warming her face. Instead, the palm she had pressed near his heart curled into a fist, gripping his flannel shirt, and she lowered her head to his.

He froze, watching her eyes until she closed them. Her lips brushed his, but he wouldn't allow the response building in his body to take over. She'd pull away, run away. Blame him. No, he kept himself in check, gave her the opportunity to pull away.

And she did. But only for a breath.

***

A heartbeat. A breath. A flutter of eyelashes...

That was all it took to change everything. All over again. Tom had frozen beneath her, but she felt the surge of his heart against the heel of her palm as her lips whispered over his. The *and* she'd been fighting against all day—

Why had she been pushing it away? She lifted her head, allowing inches between his mouth and hers. Why? Because...

Oh but, this.

She lowered her mouth again, and this time Tom met her lips. With a soft groan she could feel more than hear, he kissed her back. Tentatively at first, as if afraid she'd flit away like a frightened bird. But as she leaned into him, hesitation wore away. His ungloved hand slid against her cheek—the muddied one he'd laughed about—and then cupped the back of her head. His fingers wove into her messy braid, surely undoing whatever remained of the weave she'd fingered it into earlier.

It should have mattered that they were in a mudhole in a working pen with a calf staring at them. It didn't. It should have mattered that their lives were on different paths—his in Rock Creek and hers a promise in Texas. Nope. It really should have mattered that she'd lost respect for him a little ways back in time and hadn't wanted to be one of his mistakes, no matter what his smile did to her insides.

That did matter. Some.

No, it mattered still.

The magic crumbled, and she stilled. He responded the moment she went stiff. Fingers still twined in her hair, he froze again. His blue eyes flew open, so near that again she caught herself enamored with the dark flakes peppering the steel blue. Turmoil turned, making a mess of her mind.

"Dre..." he whispered. That voice? Tom's? Not a tone she remembered hearing from him. Gentle, yet somehow possessive. As heady and intoxicating as the kiss. It puddled her middle with warmth and fogged her mind with more confusion.

Did the past matter? Because this man looking back at her, he didn't hold the look of a player. All smirkish and confident and demanding. Instead, there in his gaze was longing, yes, but the tender sort. Also, worry. And something more she wasn't sure she could name. Or should.

What did she know though? All things considered, she was an innocent—better said, naïve—girl who only knew enough to keep away from men who'd dipped themselves into a less-than-honorable reputation. Seemed like a good policy to hold on to.

Dre scrambled to get her knees beneath her and then to her feet. Heat had taken her face captive, and as she turned away, her hands trembled. Behind her, Tom jumped to stand, and before she managed two steps of escape, his hand cupped her mud-caked elbow.

"Don't run."

Impulse wanted to ignore him and slug her way across the pen. Except, maybe not completely, because the low, gentle quality of his voice also had her heart longing to turn. To find his chest and lean against it, to feel his arms ease around her.

Is that what would happen?

"That was—" She swallowed, hating that her voice wobbled. "That was a mistake. I'm sorry."

He closed the small gap between them, keeping his hand on her arm in a light grip. "Dre, look at me."

No way. Not then. Not there. Not when she'd been weak and dumb and was likely to do it all over again the second their eyes met.

Didn't matter, because he wasn't having it. The mud squished under his booted step, and he moved around her, forcing a face-to-face. "Dre."

She shook her head, blinking, because now, dang it, there were tears. Gritting her teeth, she drew in a firm breath. She was not going to cry about this man!

His gloved hand hooked under her chin, and he tipped her face up. "Just talk to me."

The rumble of a truck lumbering down the mud-caked road filled the snowy air around them. Her out.

"I can't do this now."

Tom looked over his shoulder and then back at her. Oh, that look. Hurt and yearning and humility and that other thing she wasn't going to name. Her heart sliced open, the little throb of ache there telling.

He nodded, then stepped away, moving toward the crazy calf that had started it all.

Such a mess. One that wasn't going to clean up nearly as easily as the mud.

One, Dre decided, she'd rather avoid entirely.

Chapter Eleven

DRE FELT SURE THE FOOD WAS DELICIOUS.

It had smelled good, and Mama was a good cook, even if she didn't attempt Dre's "specialties" when Dre wasn't home. But she didn't know firsthand. She could hardly eat, and what food she did force into her mouth somehow lost its flavor between the fork and her tongue.

Turned out, avoiding someone you kissed the day before was a little bit agonizing.

Tom seemed to be himself. Maybe. Probably. She hadn't made eye contact, and other than mumbling a "happy Thanksgiving" when he'd come through the door two hours before, she hadn't spoken to him. Instead, she found things to keep occupied with in the kitchen. At the table, she chose the seat farthest from where he'd planted without facing him.

After dinner, she decided washing dishes was her new calling in life.

Keeping herself to herself felt wearisome, but she'd maintained an outward calm. She hoped.

The drive home from the river property the night before had been loaded with silence. The kind that seemed sharp and cold and exhausting. For her part. She'd shut her eyes as soon as they were out of the driveway and pretended to be asleep the whole drive. Because, heaven bless it, talking to the guy you just lip-locked with in the mud would be totally crazy.

The constant tenor of Paul and Tom's voices had filled the cab—a conversation mostly about the new manager Paul had given a test run that day, and Paul's hopes for the herd he was building on the southern property. Tom had sounded supportive. Excited for Paul.

And tired.

Surely Paul had taken that as a general tired. Not as an emotional condition.

When Dre had gotten home and out of a long, hot shower, Janelle had bounced on the bed where she'd been waiting, eyes dancing, expectation scribbled like a two-year-old's crayon all over her face.

"So..." Janelle's grin could have stretched the whole width of Texas.

Flames seemed to crawl over Dre's cheeks. She couldn't look at Janelle. "Don't ask."

"What?" The weight of the world dropped through her voice.

Dre swallowed. Could she even say it out loud? For the love, she was a horrible human being. How could she have— "I kissed him."

"What!?" It was like Janelle had a vocal trampoline. *Up, up, up, up. Down. Up...* "No way." *Down.*

The changes in her friend's pitch pretty much summed up Dre's emotions on the day.

"I kissed him. Now I can't even look at him."

"Did he kiss you back?"

Dre's lips pinned closed, and she ripped a hairbrush through her wet tresses.

"There's no way." Disbelief sagged in Janelle's *down* tone. "I swear, he was so—"

"He kissed me back." Dre whipped around to face Janelle. "But I shouldn't have kissed him in the first place. I don't want this."

"You don't want what?"

Good question. What exactly was it Dre was afraid of? Answers felt near and tangible, but not really definable. Him? She didn't want Tom? She tried that one on. Every bit of that felt wrong. Tom was...

Her heart did that achy squeeze thing that happened when you longed for something. At least, she assumed that everyone felt that achy squeeze when a yearning snagged their heart. When it came to Tommy Kent, she'd felt the squishy pain thing for too long, and it had grown significantly more intense since this little holiday reunion.

Why had he stayed in Rock Creek? It was light-years easier not to think about him, thus not feel that thing that she was feeling, when he wasn't right there in front of her. Did he know what this was—

No. Was that even possible? He knew?

She had kissed him back five years ago.

The night ended with Janelle's sympathetic pouty face, a hug, and an assurance that Dre would figure it out. At least, Janelle's night had ended there. As tired as Dre had been from a full day of working cattle—and that was no small deal—her mind continued to tie her heart into knots long past the silence that followed lights-out.

And now? Thanksgiving dinner had been served, consumed, and cleaned. Paul and Tom were doing something in the other room, and Dre didn't know what to do with herself as the last dish landed safely on the shelf.

"Who's up for Pitch?" Paul wandered into the kitchen, deck of cards in hand.

Since Daddy and Mama had declared that it was Turkey Day nap time, Tom wasn't in sight, and Janelle had disappeared as well, Dre assumed Paul was asking her.

So now what? Pitch was a four-person game. With partners. Conversation and eye contact would be unavoidable without some pretty strenuous and obvious effort.

"Sure." What else could she do? "You and me?"

"You're going to make your friend partner with a virtual stranger?"

"Oh." Right. That'd be rude. Why hadn't she thought of that? Too focused on *not* being Tom's partner. "No, that was dumb. I'll play with Janelle. I doubt she's ever played before, so be nice."

Paul studied her with a suspicious look. "You okay, kid?"

"Yep." Oh. That hit a high note. Yikes. "Why?"

His eyebrows lifted, and he kept on looking as if he could see inside her mind. But he only shook his head.

Janelle resurfaced, and the three of them moved to the dining table, where Tom was already sitting.

"Is it on?" he asked.

"Yep." Paul pulled a chair out across from Tom and slid onto it. "But Dre's scared. Says we have to play nice."

"That is not what I said."

Paul snorted. "Exactly what you said. You said be nice."

"We're always nice." Tom winked at her.

Heat crashed over Dre. She slid her attention from the man on her left speedy-like and focused it on Janelle. "We don't have to play if you don't want to." *Please don't want to.*

"I love Pitch." Janelle settled onto the chair across the table and tossed a sassy smirk at Paul. "And by all means, *don't* be nice. I most certainly won't be."

"Oh!" Paul laughed, tapping the deck of cards on the table. "It is on."

And so it began. Two hours of cards, competition, and for Dre, a weird vacillating between having a ball and feeling every tied-up, mixed-up, fueled-up emotion about the man on her left. Whom she'd kissed. And had kissed her back.

But she hadn't meant it. Or shouldn't have meant it. Or...

The last hand was hers. She focused on the cards, waited for the final card to land, and then reached for her win. Victory.

Tom's hand landed overtop hers. The warm, calloused palm smothered all her knuckles as his fingers wrapped around hers. The world stopped. Froze right there—no more rotating, revolving, or tilting. There was his hand and hers, and electricity pulsed through that connection. His eyes on her. His mouth, the corners bowing up. And her heart doing a little welcome-home dance inside her chest.

For him.

"What are you doing?"

Dre blinked. Dying. In a good way. That was what she was doing. Did he mean that?

"Dre." Paul cleared his voice. "That hand is Tom's."

Exactly. Wait. "What?"

"You didn't take that hand. Thief." Paul gave her shoulder a playful shove. The small push moved her hand, and contact slipped from Tom's.

The world began a slow restart. She would nearly swear she could actually hear it groan as the planet began its ancient spin all over again. Dre glanced at the cards—yes, that was what they'd been doing, playing cards—and retraced her mental steps back to where she'd left off before she'd gone into an alternate reality. Before Tom's hand had smothered her whole world.

There was her joker that should have taken the hand. Covered by the king of hearts.

Wide-eyed, she peeked at Tom.

He met her eyes as if he'd been waiting patiently all day for her to connect with his. "That one's mine."

***

Waiting wasn't Tom's thing. It was awkward and frustrating and, well, hard.

That had been true pretty much his whole life. How many suppers had he spoiled because he *couldn't wait another second* and had found some kind of junk filler to snack on? Or how about speeding tickets had he accumulated? More than he'd admit to, because waiting to get places by going the speed limit was intolerable.

Waiting to have sex? Yeah, didn't do that one either. One of the bigger reasons Dre had lost respect for him. Wasn't sure— they didn't talk about those things back then.

So this thing with Dre was a little bit of torture, and not something he'd built up any kind of endurance for. But he'd spent the last four years wondering if she'd come home. Wondering if she'd ever look at him again. What was a day full of food and friends and her working ridiculously hard to avoid him with that backdrop? Probably good practice, that was what.

But when she peeked up at him, all timidity and shock in her eyes, backlit by a beautiful blush the roots of which he knew exactly, waiting suddenly made sense. Because she'd just melted and couldn't hide it. For him.

He could become a much more patient man for a lifetime of that.

Chapter Twelve

BLUE SKIES SET THE BACKDROP FOR THE BARN IN THE MIDDLE OF TOWN, BUT THE AIR REMAINED COLD.

Dre's breath puffed white against the crisp morning, as did Janelle's. Together they laid out the twinkle lights, attaching the labels Janelle had helped Dre make the night before. They designated reels of lights for the two trees flanking the barn, for the windows on the front and side, for the gambrel roofline, and the last set for the interior of the barn, where Dre had planned to create a little wonderland of joy.

Later that night, the festivities would begin. They'd have a Hallmark-esque lighting ceremony, only for the barn, not a Christmas tree. Then the kids would break the piñata—Mama was at home making it, and Dre had weaseled Daddy into filling it with her later. This year it'd be a simple square—a replica of a Christmas present. In future years she'd get more complicated, when she had more time to pull things together. After the piñata, a barn dance, because who didn't like a barn dance? Even if one didn't dance, a barn dance was awesome.

It was all coming together. Her festive little dream for Rock Creek's town barn. The vision in her head about to spring to life, thanks to Paul and Tom.

Dre paused and straightened from the piles of lights she had laid out on the park table. Gazing into the clear blue sky, at the moment so deep and beautiful it made her want to reach for it to check that it was real, she let her heart swim in gratitude. She shut her eyes and smiled in the glow of the yellow morning sun.

The familiar rumble of Paul's big ol' pickup pulled her back to the task ahead, but the curve on her mouth stayed soft. How could it not? This day was nearly perfect, and it'd only just started. Paul and Tom both hopped out of the blue Ford, two doors popping shut one right after another. Her bother wore his Carhartt work coat and a Huskers stocking cap. Tom had on a black ski coat and gray beanie. As they each grabbed a ladder from the back of Paul's pickup, Dre couldn't help watching Tom.

He moved with ease, lifting the extension ladder as if it were nothing. Glimpses of the boy he'd been quickly vanished as she watched the man he'd become. Confident, strong, directed. And yet, as he glanced at her, relaxed at the mouth and gentle in the eyes, he was kindness and patience.

Love is patient. Love is kind. Look for those qualities, bumpkin-girl. They're so much more important than a boy being cute or popular.

Wise words from Mama, sprouting in her mind like spring tulips on this chilly day. Rooting in places already cultivated in her heart.

"Good day to build dreams, eh, Dre?" Tom leaned the ladder against a nearby ash tree whose branches were spindly and interesting without their green cover of summer.

Tom's low tone wrapped around her, and she couldn't help a smile. She straightened from her organizing and turned to him. "Did I say thank you yet?"

"For what?"

With slow measure, she cast her look over the barn, a thrill building ever more inside. Tonight. She'd see what she envisioned in real life. Her first live project. "This." Her smile felt whimsical as she found his face again.

He stared at her, mouth lifted in a soft grin that turned her belly deliciously warm. There was magic there, and the lights weren't even up. Magic in the space between him and her, and suddenly she wished there wasn't space at all.

"Do you want us to start on the roofline or the trees?" Paul's question, called from the spot where he'd placed his ladder by the barn, broke the spell.

Dre swallowed, her mind warring between ignoring her brother, whose unintentional interruption brought reality creeping back, and grabbing on to his distraction to put distance between Tom and herself.

She couldn't avoid Tom. She'd tried the day before, and it'd been exhausting, not to mention futile. By the end of the evening, before Tom and Paul left, she'd been right back to what had unraveled her before. Tom's patient, quiet persistence undid her.

Was undoing her.

"Let's do the barn, since you're already there." Dre turned toward Paul, giving Tom her back and regaining sense as she did so.

She snagged her mental list of reasons why Tommy Kent couldn't continue prying into her heart. They were on different life tracts. That was the biggest, most rational reason. She was going back to Texas. Leaving the very next morning, for heaven's sake. He was staying right there in Rock Creek, apparently for the rest of his life, because he loved the land and the people. Noncongruent plans. So.

Buried underneath, there was the other thing. The one she'd tried to leave unwritten. Or erased. The one about her being disappointed in what he'd become in high school. Maybe even mad.

Such mangled emotions, brewing up inside her and ruining a good day.

No, they wouldn't. She didn't have to let them. The four of them had work to do, and Paul had called a few others who were willing to come help. She'd have a crew to direct in no time, and all sorts of glorious fun was to be had. Who needed mangled emotions?

With lots of pointing and explanations, she set Paul up with the high parts of the barn. Janelle molded herself into the plan by delivering reels of lights and feeding them foot by foot as Paul scrambled up and down the ladder. Dre put Tom onto the trees, and when Haley arrived, she took over for Janelle as Paul's light feeder, and Janelle joined Tom at the trees, leaving Dre to lay out the interior plan to the other three who'd shown up for twinkle-light duty.

The groups chatted and laughed, and Dre felt a light sense of pride as she watched the interaction. This was community—as beautiful as the lights were sure to be that night. For all her visions of structure and function, it was the interaction that thrilled her the most. Grinning, she snatched the pair of pruning shears and strode toward a wind row of pine trees.

For close to an hour, she inspected and snipped, pruning evergreen boughs from the bottoms of the layered trees in a way that wouldn't be noticeable in the wind row once she was done. Tom and Janelle arrived where she was working as she finished adding to the pile of branches she'd created.

"Do you want these at the table where we put the wire frames?" Janelle started gathering the boughs.

"Yes. Should be enough for six wreaths, I hope."

Janelle nodded, added two more branches to her armload, and started back for the picnic table. Tom layered a pile of boughs in his arm as well.

"Six wreaths?" he asked.

"Yeah, one for each of the windows that face Main Street, and two for the big double front doors." Dre crawled out from her crouched-under-the-tree position and smiled.

Tom laughed.

"What?"

He stepped nearer. "You could pass for a pine with all the needles you've collected."

"Oh." She shuffled the pruners and the branches she'd clipped into one hand so that she had a hand free to run through the hair lying beneath her stocking cap. Her fingers caught on the tresses. Sticky.

Tom chuckled again. "Here." He set the branches down, pulled his gloves off, and pried strands of hair from the sap smothered on her fingers. The grin on his mouth grew as he freed her hair from her fingers and then picked evergreen needles from the strands.

"Seems I'm always in a mess when you're around," Dre said.

He shrugged, stopped grooming her hair, and tipped her chin up, then to one side, followed by the other. "You look good to me."

Magic again. Her belly fluttered as a charge ran through her chest and over her arms. Why was he so dang charming? Was this how he talked to all the girls she'd seen him with? That thought doused the magic, and she stepped back. Tom let his hand fall away. She caught the fade of his smile, the dimming of the dance in his blue eyes, before he bent to retrieve the branches he'd set aside.

She cleared her throat, searched her mind for something to say that would be both safe and would rescue them from the awkwardness of her subtle rejection. They finished gathering the pine boughs and started back toward the barn.

"Your nice ski coat is going to get covered in sap," she said, relieved to have *something* to say. "What happened to your work coat?"

"Mud." He looked at her, a smirk playing on the corners of his mouth. "Well, likely not just mud."

His wink tugged a chuckle from her as she remembered the comment she'd made the day before last that had sent them both laughing. The one she'd made before she kissed him.

Tom paused and reached a gloved hand to catch Dre's elbow, halting her trail toward the others and turning her to face him. "Dre, I need to talk to you."

It was tempting to get lost in the depths of the gaze he kept on her. Sincere, and so full of that something she couldn't— wouldn't—define. The moment and feeling would have been beautiful. Perfect, even. Except for that mental list she'd pulled up earlier of the reasons that this thing—this magic between them—was a bad idea.

In the three seconds that passed, her throat swelled to near closure. "Please don't." She pushed the words out in a whisper she hadn't intended to sound harsh.

The light in his gaze dimmed, but strangely, the depth and emotion didn't. He held her there for another breath, studying her as if he understood, was battling to accept, and ultimately wanted her smile more than anything. Though the sting of rejection clearly scrawled on his expression, the line of his mouth relaxed, and he nodded.

He squeezed her arm and let her go. Side by side in an achy silence, they returned to the group.

***

Quitting wasn't really his thing either.

He'd graduated at the top of their class because of straight-up determination. Finished his degree in three years with the same tenacity. And he was standing there in Rock Creek for the same reason. When it came to going for what he wanted, he was relentless.

Tom stayed at the park the rest of the day, working alongside Dre and the rest of the little crew they'd put together. The barn and the area around it became the wonderland Dre had promised the city council. Not that he was surprised. It was a little bit of magic though.

Dre continued to work, all smiles and laughter. Often forced. She might be shocked to know he could tell the difference. He could in a heartbeat. But she did cover her emotions fairly well—he doubted anyone else knew that her heart was in turmoil.

So maybe on this, he should give up. She was clearly determined to keep the electricity between them grounded. Or snuffed out entirely. After all, she was leaving the next day. Maybe she was right.

He knew what would happen to him though. Dre would sit right there in his heart, possessing his mind like the best dream, and keeping him locked in a hope that was probably unreasonable and unfounded. He knew because she already had.

If he told her, would she believe him?

Didn't seem to matter. Apparently she wasn't going to give him the chance.

Chapter Thirteen

"I'VE SEEN MULES WITH MORE SENSE THAN YOU."

Janelle sidled up next to Dre, her face flushed with laughter.

The night, by all accounts, including the delight on Janelle's face, was a total success. Yellow-white lights twinkled from the barn rafters with a happy, romantic celebration as the majority of the town's folk moved through the warm space, faces wreathed in smiles and hands full of hot cider or cookies. Several times a neighbor or friend had stopped near her to pat her on the shoulder with a *love this* or *the barn is beautiful* or *such a perfect idea.*

Dre did a little internal *woo-hoo* dance, and the smile stretched on her face was genuine, even if there was something in the area of her heart that felt stiff and cold. That area in her chest was easier to ignore when Janelle wasn't picking at it.

She met Janelle's accusation with a head-on look. "You stopped making the rounds, teaching your Texas-style line dances, and generally flirting to come tell me that I'm stubborn?"

"I'm not flirting." Janelle's smile brimmed, and she winked. "Much. Just a little stock inspecting, is all. And that's not the topic anyway." She dropped an arm around Dre's shoulders and angled her in a way that put Tom directly in Dre's line of sight.

She hadn't needed help finding him, thank you very much. She'd known exactly where Tom was. Far corner of the barn, keeping mostly to himself. A few dances here and there—when one of the local girls sauntered over and asked. She knew because she couldn't *not* know. The irrational jealousy clawing within her let her know *every time* he wove onto the dance floor with a pretty new partner, and the unbreakable though invisible tether she seemed to have acquired as to his whereabouts let her know exactly where he was when he wasn't dancing.

Not that she was watching. On purpose. Or cared. Much.

"Seems a shame that such a handsome man would sequester himself in a dark corner like that." Janelle's drawl made the words *man* sound extra sexy and *sequester* like something interesting and foreign.

For the love. Dre pinned Janelle with irritation. "Of the two of us standing here, I am not the mule."

"For such a nice girl, you're sure in a horn-tossin' mood when it comes to him. You know that?"

"I told you why," Dre said.

"Girl. How can you be as bright as a shiny new penny and still insist on huggin' a rosebush?"

Dre felt her eyebrows scrunch together even as a laugh bundled in her chest. "If I knew what that meant, I'm sure I could give you an answer."

"Means you're being dumb." Janelle jutted her chin toward Tom. "Whatever he may have been or done before, he's not the rooster you hold him to be. Look at that. Keeps glancing at you like the moon hid behind the clouds and he's aching for its glow. Have you ever seen heartbreak look that dignified? Come on now and tell me that doesn't do a little something to your heart."

Dre rolled her eyes. "He's not heartbroken."

"Yeah, and you're not stubborn." One dark eyebrow pushed toward her thick corkscrew curls. "Or a little bit heart-nipped yourself, *Hungry Eyes*."

With a shrug and a playful push, Dre disengaged Janelle's arm. "Go find a cowboy to dance with, crazy woman. Leave me and my confused heart alone."

"Not until you promise you'll give him one dance."

"Not happening."

"You'll regret it. And I dare you."

"Still not happening."

Janelle crossed her arms and tilted her head into the sassiest, troublemaker look ever. "I double-dog dare you."

Dre had no notion of the limits of Janelle's Texafied expressions, but she was familiar with the double-dog dare. It was a throw down. A no-outter. A challenge good southern folk whose bellies weren't a streak of pathetic yellow didn't walk away from. Who knew why.

"What could possibly go wrong?" Janelle leaned closer, nudging Dre's arm as her voice dropped to a whisper. "Might even fall in love."

That is exactly what could go wrong. Dre slapped a mental hand over the unbidden thought. "Fine," she said instead. "One dance. And then you'll let it be?"

Janelle nodded. "Let the chips fall where they may."

"I'm gonna need a pinkie on that."

Hand up, Janelle smile victoriously. When Dre hooked her right pinkie with hers, Janelle squeezed. "Pinkie promise, but it has to be a full dance, and you have to look him in those blue eyes at least once."

Dre grunted a laugh. "I'm sure that'll do it."

"Pretty sure what's done is done." She winked again and sauntered away. Certainly to find Travis or Wyatt or Chuck, any of whom would gladly follow her onto the dance floor.

Should have warned her to stay away from Chuck. Not that Janelle wouldn't be able to pick out trouble as clearly labelled as that overgrown child. He practically wore a *toxic if handled* warning label on his velvet black Stetson. Something Janelle could pick out easily and was smart enough to take heed. Shelby Rice, however, had marked her territory on the beast long before they'd graduated high school, and though the man-child was slow about putting a ring on it, he was *hers*, and everyone in Rock Creek knew it, even if he did have a knack for boiling Shelby's jealous temper.

Ah well. Janelle was as street smart as she was versed in quirky clichés. She'd figure it out. Plus, she'd pushed Dre into this...whatever this was about to be. She might deserve a little discomfort of her own.

Though Dre had to force her booted feet to move, once she was in motion, she seemed drawn to Tom like metal shavings to a charged magnet. Standing aloof in the corner, hands shoved in his denim pockets, and a gray-striped button-down stretched over his work-formed shoulders, she had to admit he cut a handsome profile. Actually she'd already admitted—several times over—that Tommy Kent was handsome. Always had been. Part of the problem right there.

He glanced her direction when she'd made it a few feet from his planted position. The apple of his tanned cheek lifted as one corner of his mouth poked upward. Dre wove through the three people separating them, and heat trickled over her arms as he turned toward her.

Eye contact. Check. Now that that part of the obligation was fulfilled, she could look elsewhere. Anytime. Like now. Or later...

"There's the beautiful genius behind all this." He pulled his left hand from his pocket and grazed her elbow, forearm, and palm with his fingertips. "I was wondering if you'd be avoiding me all night."

Fire flared on her cheeks. "I—" She swallowed. Tried again. "I wasn't...I mean I...um..."

With the right hand he'd disentangled from his other pocket, he lightly pinched her lips together. "No lying to me,

Dre."

"What?"

"Let's start there, how 'bout? Wherever this dance goes and anything after that, you're going to be honest with me, and I'm going to be honest with you."

"We're not dancing."

"Isn't that what you came over here for? Because Janelle told you that you had to give me one dance?"

How in the cold white winter did he know that?

"I like Janelle." He smiled. Not big, and only mildly flirtatious, but his mouth bowed upward in a way that settled her awkwardness a bit.

"Uh. Yeah. Janelle is kind of Texas personified. Unique, big personality. Sometimes scary. But mostly just awesome."

Tom chuckled but didn't say anything to that. Instead, he studied her, blue eyes tracing the curve of her face and reflecting a depth that began to stretch in her disobedient heart.

"You gonna ask me?"

She didn't have to and she knew it. She slipped her hand into his rough, calloused palm, and he stepped toward the crowded dance floor. He held her like a gentleman, warm arm curled around her shoulder and back, leaving enough space between them that those who cared to look would have plenty of room to speculate whether or not this dance meant any more to either of them than a pair of old friends sharing a meaningless dance.

Which was exactly what it was, for clarity's sake.

Of course Allison Krause would be singing "When You Say Nothing at All" to muddy everything up. Between the lights overhead—Dre's idea, the barn-turned-Christmas wonderland—and the handsome man she'd been crushing on forever pouring his attention solely on her, why not add romantic music? That way she'd have no chance to survive this double-dog-dare dance with her head on straight and heart fully intact. It was like heaven conspired against her.

Huh. Interesting that—she'd never once asked God what He thought about any of this Tommy Kent confusion. Surely, though, if she did, God would tell her exactly what she'd thought before—she and Tom were a bad idea. Because...

Well. Just because.

So. She'd better get some things cleared up.

"Tom, I should apologize." She rushed the words, only giving him a graze of eye contact as she barreled through the rest. "I'm sorry about the other day. I shouldn't have—I mean, I don't know what I was doing. Thinking. But, umm, I shouldn't have..."

"Kissed me?"

Her heart hammered, the pulse throbbing heat over her face, her ears, even her hands. She swallowed, forcing herself to peek at him again.

He shook his head, a slow, certain movement, as his steady stare claimed all her attention. "I'm not accepting that apology."

"What?" Her lips parted as the word came out in a breath.

"Whatever you choose to do with this thing between us, Dre, you need to know that I don't regret it. Least of all, that kiss."

Holy smokes, he could lean down, right there in front of all of Rock Creek, and claim her lips, and she'd melt into him. How could a man wield that kind of magic?

The art of a player.

The thought cracked through her mesmerized mind, crushing the swell of heart-shaped possibilities. Why would he play *her* though? He knew, didn't he, that she'd never be that kind of girl? He knew, didn't he, what she thought of that kind of guy?

What was he after?

She blinked, suddenly aware of how her forehead had

furrowed, how her eyebrows had pushed together. Aware that he probably saw her confusion—the war between emotion and mistrust. And yet, he said nothing.

"Why are you here, Tom?" Though her voice was quiet, only enough for the two of them to hear, it layered the words with more questions than face value. "Why did you stay?"

"To see you again." No hesitancy. Not even a breath to consider his answer or the impact it might have on her. On them.

She squared her gaze with his, almost daring him to play her. To say sweet things he didn't mean.

He continued to hold her eyes, and there was no falsehood there. She remembered the deal he'd laid out before this dance had begun. No lies between them. He'd be honest, and he expected her to be too. Even at the expense of dignity.

"I didn't come back to Rock Creek for this," she said. Why, she wasn't sure, except that it was the truth.

"I know. But the thing is, you're in my head, and I needed to see you again."

His thumb ran over her wrist, traced the outside of her palm, and then over her knuckles. The feathering touch sent pleasure through her arm, over her shoulders, and sinking into her heart. Walls she'd been determined to maintain crumbled like dry sand, and she stepped into him, leaning her forehead against his chest. He tucked her hand near his heart, covered it with his own.

"I'm glad you're happy in Texas, Dre."

The deep tenor of his voice so near her ear made the skin along her neck prickle.

"Don't think for a minute I'm trying to take that from you. So if that's why you're sorry—"

"It's not."

Did he really want honesty? She moved away enough to look up at him. He nodded, a painful knowing in his eyes, but also an invitation. A silent *tell me.*

And suddenly there it was. The anger she'd clutched toward him, sitting right next to the affection she'd tried hard not to cultivate. That look—the one that said he knew why she fought this, accepted her hurt even if it wasn't completely justified, and wanted her to say it—somehow provoked an icy resentment the strength of which surprised her. It hadn't always been that powerful, had it?

There she was, seventeen again, and furious with the boy who'd kissed her, because she couldn't trust that he was sincere. That hurt deeply, because she'd liked him so much and used to think he could be the moon in her someday sky. Turned out, he'd just been a boy who'd done stupid stuff.

Dre clamped her jaw, certain that if she said what was building in her mind, she'd regret it. Not only that she'd shame him, hurt him, but that she'd expose an ugliness in herself she'd rather no one know about.

Ms. Krause finished her *say nothing at all* lyrics, which was ironic. Or was it prophetic? Dre didn't know. At the moment, it was frustrating. Even so, when the next song—another crooning heartthrob—started, Tom tucked her close and continued to move to the slow rhythm of the music.

And she let him.

Chapter Fourteen

Velvet black stretched soft and rich overhead, the
smattering of diamonds winking their last overture
before the sun would draw a curtain on them.

Tom stood at the east-facing window of his small rental,
mug of hot coffee in hand, and waited for the next act of the
cosmos. Sunrise was still a solid hour away, but the early hour
was normal for him. Not sleeping, however, was not. Well,
hadn't been, prior to this week.

Scenes from the previous days rolled through his mind, every
one of them with Dre. Her shy smile when he'd first seen her
again. After years of only ever seeing those blue eyes and that
beautiful face in his memory, that little lift of her perfect
mouth hit him breathless and nearly put him on his knees.
Every moment with her after—even the ones where she was
working herself into a headache trying to avoid him—had
needled into his heart, fastening her there a little more
securely.

Did he love her? If Paul was there, being nosey yet again,
Tom would have to own it. Yeah. He loved her, and it kind of
hurt.

Last night, when they moved from the dance floor, her
hand wrapped in his, she looked up at him again, and he'd
known she was ready to be honest. He'd grabbed her white

winter coat and his black ski jacket, waited while she pushed her arms into the sleeves, covering the deep teal sweater that made her eyes look like a tropical ocean paradise, and then walked beside her toward one of the lit-up ash trees. Outside the barn, a few kids scattered hither and thither, running, tossing snow, laughing. Loving Dre's inspired creation as much as the adults keeping warm inside.

She'd done this. Did she know how awesome that was? Brought the whole community together in a way that felt joyful and natural and perfect. Not many places had that. Rock Creek didn't before. And now? This was only the beginning— he felt sure. She thought she'd brought them a few twinkle lights and wreaths. A lit-up barn. It was so much more. She'd breathed a fresh sense of community right into the middle of town. And it was infused with her—determination and kindness, a sense of beauty and love.

She amazed him, and she didn't even know it.

Kind of like those days back in high school. She'd loved Paul with raw stubbornness, even though her brother was a certified disaster who'd split her heart. Tom knew how it tore her up to see him sent away—thinking that Paul was locked into a life that would forever be chaos, and wanting so much more for him.

Watching her muscle through it that last year had made Tom ache, often kept him up at night, and worse, made him feel entirely useless. Because he had no idea how to help. Even if he did know, by then he was pretty sure she'd reject it from him. If he'd paid more attention before, he'd have been able to walk with her though all of it when certainly she'd felt terribly alone, and maybe would have had a better idea of what to do. But he hadn't. Been too busy living for himself. Not a whole lot different from Paul.

They reached a semi-lit spot under the tree where a picnic table sat dusted with frost. He leaned against the tabletop, making their heights nearly the same, and watched while she sorted through the things she wanted to say. When her forehead furrowed again, he reached to finger the thick wheat-colored hair that lay along her cheek, tucking it behind her ear.

"I'm not fragile, Dre. Just say it."

She drew a breath, a painful scowl molding her eyebrows. "You..." Another breath. Pain tightened into anger. "You disappointed me. And I'm still not Abigail."

Shutting her eyes, she stepped back and tucked her chin into her coat. A stuttered sigh left her mouth in a puff of cold white. "I'm sorry. That's stupid and unfair. It was a long time ago and not really any of my business."

"It's your business."

Her chin lifted, and he read misery and confusion in her eyes. "No, it wasn't. And I don't know why—"

"Dre." He reached for her hand and tugged her toward him. "I'm sorry. I'm sorry I was that guy. And I'm sorry for the stuff you had to deal with alone."

Once again her eyes pinched, the expression pain and anger and frustration. All focused on him? He didn't think so, but maybe? *Choices have consequences.* His mother used to tell them that—him and his brother. Usually after they'd done something stupid. Like setting the living room floor on fire seeing if they could make a spark "like cavemen"—with two sticks and friction. Against all odds, they'd succeeded, and then had to work all summer to pay for new carpet.

Choices have consequences—and sometimes you were too wrapped up in yourself to understand that those consequences didn't always fall right away, or even on your own shoulders. One choice, and then another, and now here he was. Watching the consequences play out in Dre.

Would it matter if he told her the rumors were exaggerated? That the truth was it'd only been Abigail? Seemed like that might be a defensive stance.

So, what then? He waited for her anger, prepared to take it from her. Instead, she nodded, her expression locking into some kind of self-disciplined stoicism that actually cut into his heart more than her anger would have.

"Dre?"

"It's history." Her voice seemed distant and a little cold. "And shouldn't matter."

"But—"

"The thing is, Tom, I don't see how this would work."

His heart squeezed. "Why?"

"Because I live, like, thirteen hours away."

"And?"

"That's not really practical, and I think…"

He waited. Dre tucked her chin into her coat again, hiding her expression. When her eyes squeezed shut, he stood, slid a palm against her cold cheek. She leaned into his hand as another shaky breath puffed white from her lips. Stepping closer, he wrapped an arm around her shoulders and sighed a sort of sad relief when she leaned against him.

They stayed that way until the cold of the November night sank through his ski coat. Dre shivered, and he resigned to the undefined between them.

"You leave tomorrow."

Her head moved against him in a nod. "In the morning. I'm scheduled to work Sunday afternoon, and classes start again on Monday."

"Working and a full-time student. Ambitious much?"

"School doesn't pay for itself."

It surprised him a little that she'd pay her own way. Shouldn't have. That was Dre—and with Paul's fiascos, her parents' money probably went other places. Not that any of it was his business. But a balloon of pride in her puffed in his chest. Ambitious. Determined. Kind. Joyful. Talented. That was his Dre.

Except, she really wasn't his.

"I'd better start shutting things down in there." Dre stepped away and pointed toward the barn.

Tom nodded, a feeling of awkwardness pushing insecurity through him. He'd help her clean up. Then...

Goodbye?

That hadn't settled right. And by the time they had things restored and the lit barn secured, the small group of them—Paul, Haylee, Janelle, Dre, and himself—had stood in a loose circle chatting for a few minutes before they'd broken apart and headed home.

Might explain the not-sleeping-well thing.

An orange-yellow edged the eastern horizon. Tom turned from the window and from the replay that had rolled out in slow-mo in his mind. He moved to his tiny kitchen and set his empty mug in the sink. That couldn't be it. Just...it couldn't be.

He walked across the still-dark living room to the small desk he had smashed up against a far wall. Though he was organized—didn't much like messes—his house was all function and no form. Dre likely would frown. Feel uninspired and flat within his walls. Clearly he needed help making things work. Hers.

Way to jump the gun, cowboy. The woman is leaving town.

He flicked on the desk lamp and opened the drawer where he had a small ream of lined paper. Sliding onto the no-frills chair sitting cockeyed in front of the work space, he snatched a pen from a cracked *Class of 2000* mug and put ink to page.

It took about eight starts, seven of which found their way into the fireplace as freshly crumpled balls, before the right words scrawled out. Maybe they were the right words. There weren't very many of them.

Clearly he wasn't a poet.

Actually, he wasn't much of anything. Just a simple country man who loved his hometown. His dreams weren't impressive, and he didn't have a whole lot to offer. But he did love her. Maybe that would matter?

The question gnawed unanswered, but he pulled on a clean pair of jeans and shirt, pushed a worn hat over his head, and shoved his arms into the sleeves of his freshly cleaned Carhartt. He'd stop at Ms. Mays, and hopefully his timing would be right.

With a deep breath and enough courage to get by, he slipped the blank envelope containing his heart into his coat pocket and headed for the door.

***

"I'll grab us some coffee." Janelle unbuckled her seat belt and reached for the door handle.

Dre nodded behind a massive yawn. Goodness, sleep would have been good. They had a long drive, and she was currently behind the wheel. Probably not the best setup, but she didn't want to tell Janelle that she'd lain awake all night, because then she'd have to tell her why, and that was a slippery slope.

At some point, she and Janelle would switch, and then Dre could sleep. Maybe.

As if he hadn't spent enough time in her head all through the night, Tom pulled up to the station in his white Ford pickup and cut the engine. Dre climbed out of her little Camry as he hopped from the driver's seat and strode toward her car, brown bag dangling from his right hand and a look pinned straight on her like she might hold his forever.

Maybe that last part was her exhausted, overly dramatic imagination.

"Hey."

One corner of his mouth twitched upward. "Morning."

"Morning. What are you doing here?"

He studied her, and without thought, she stepped closer. His fingers found that lock of hair that always seemed to find its way over her cheek and tucked it behind her ear. "Didn't say goodbye."

"Oh."

He lifted the brown bag. "These are fresh. Janelle's not allergic to nuts, I hope."

Dre breathed a small laugh. "That would be ironic, since she's a little bit nuts herself. What are they?"

"Ms. May's cinnamon buns."

"Is she even open this early?"

"No. But she likes me, so..."

Sweet. And cute. Also, why was there a pain in her chest that maybe wasn't entirely painful?

Tom turned to the gas pump, tugged his wallet from his back pocket, and pulled out a card.

"You don't have to do that."

"I know."

"Tom."

Even when she touched his elbow, he ignored her pathetic argument. The scanner read his card, and when the *begin fueling* flashed on the screen, he started the pump and then turned back to her.

"You're missed around here, you know? And now, now you're legendary."

She laughed. "Legendary? Why's that?"

"The girl with the big dreams?"

"Yeah, no one says that."

"I do."

Rolling her hands into the sleeves of her cream-colored sweater, she played with the cuffs and tried to think what to say. *This won't work.* How did she know? *I'm too scared to try.* Why? *Because I'm afraid you'll disappoint me again.*

Was that true? Here he'd been nothing but nearly perfect to her all week, and that was the measure of her thoughts about him? All he was now was what he'd been for a few brief months in high school? What was wrong with her?

"Do you still not accept my apology?" She wasn't sure where the question came from, but she worked up the courage to look at him, knowing that the mixed-up hope she had latched on to probably played clearly on her face.

"No."

A tiny smile slipped onto her mouth, and he matched it.

The gas slurped through the hose, and then the pump banged to a stop. Time was about up, right about the moment she was ready to wave the white flag.

Tom ignored the pump. "Are you going to answer if I call you?"

"If you call." She lifted her eyebrows in challenge.

He laughed, shaking his head. "You'll see, Dre. You'll see."

His hand swallowed hers, still tucked into her sweater, and he tugged her into a hug. After a breath of hesitation, she slid her free arm through his and over his shoulder. In silence, they held on, and it felt a little bit like it was a moment before they were about to dive out of a plane. Dre wondered if Tom felt the same—and if he knew what he was doing.

She sure didn't.

"You'll call me when you get there, right?" Tom pulled away, touched her face.

"Yeah."

He studied her again, and she wished she could read his thoughts. Wondered if he could read hers. He seemed certain. Set. She felt shaky. Like all her well-designed plans were under revision.

That could be resolved. She could call him tonight and tell him this wasn't going to work. She wasn't willing to try.

The thought felt sharp and jagged. More, it seemed...wrong?

At the squeak of hinges coming from the door to the Kwik-Stop, Tom leaned closer, brushed her forehead with his lips, and let her go. She stepped away, a bundle of shivers and confusion while he replaced the pump nozzle and her gas cap.

"Morning, Janelle."

"Hey there, Tom. Good to see you."

Tom smiled at Janelle, tapped the top of Dre's car, then squeezed Dre's hand one last time. "You girls be safe."

"You bet." Janelle tucked one of the two coffees she carried into the crook of her elbow, then opened her car door. "It was sure nice to meet you."

He dipped a nod, said the same back to her, and looked back down at Dre. When she thought he'd lean down for her mouth, he feathered the pad of his thumb over her bottom lip, leaving a longing that would ride with her all the way back to Texas.

"I expect to hear from you, Dre."

With a backward step, he moved toward his pickup. A chill settled in the spot where he'd been, and Dre watched him walk away.

She wasn't sure, but more likely than not, he'd done just swiped her heart and made a mess of her plans.

Chapter Fifteen

"Pretty sure you're mad at me."

They'd barely gone through the one stoplight in town before Janelle opened up the silent topic they'd been avoiding since last night.

"Look, I'm real sorry, Dre. I didn't mean to push you into something that was going to hurt. Honest. I really thought I saw sparks between you two. The good kind."

Dre loosened her grip on the steering wheel and reached to grab Janelle's hand. "You did. And I'm not mad."

"You didn't sleep. Which, by the way, isn't a good setup for driving. You should let me drive."

"Coffee will help." Dre lifted the to-go cup to her mouth, letting the steam condensate on her top lip.

"You are upset though."

"I'm..." Dre took a sip, buying a moment to sift through her thoughts. Wasn't enough. "I'm kind of turned inside out. But that's not really your fault. I would be anyway."

"There's more backstory between you two than what you told, isn't there?"

"Not really. Not much." Dre glanced at Janelle, and her shoulders slumped. "You're gonna think it's so dumb."

"What?"

"Why I'm torn up about him. Besides the distance between

us."

"Why?"

"I like him. I've always liked him."

"Yeah. Even the chickens under the front porch knew that."

Dre about spit out her coffee. "Where do you keep getting these? I mean, you're from Houston, right?"

"Mama's from Texarkana. Can't wash that kind of upbringing out with concrete."

"Holy moley, you're too much."

Janelle laughed. "Okay, comedy tactic has been successful. Now back to the serious stuff. What's got you so twisted up you don't know dirt from sky?"

Dre would rather they went back to Janelle's hilarious way with words and other fun stuff. The truth was, Dre knew Janelle's story. Her childhood. Abused before she could even understand the word, by a member of her household who was respected in their church and community. Janelle's life was all proper and silk on the outside. Total madness behind closed doors. Who was Dre to complain about the little sliver in her heart when she was sitting next to super-survivor girl?

"You know..." Janelle placed her coffee in the console holder and twisted in her seat to face Dre better. "Here's what I think you're thinking. You're thinking that you know my story, and it's such a hot, holy mess that whatever it is you're wrestling doesn't amount to dust on the piano."

Uh, nailed it. Dre glanced at her again, fighting the warm glaze in her eyes.

"But that's just competition turned sour."

"What?"

"When people compare their lives—the good or the bad— sometimes it's toxic. Like, I think when people hear my story, they think to themselves, *My crap isn't that crappy, so I guess I shouldn't worry about it.* Or something like that. Sometimes, it's good to get perspective. But I think that getting perspective and ignoring pain aren't the same thing. Pain is something we're supposed to take to our good God in heaven, no matter the size or reason. Let Him sort it out. When you don't, it's kind of like telling God, 'I've got this little thing. You mind the big stuff. I'll handle it.' Or maybe like telling a doctor, 'It's only a little cancer. You worry yourself about the big ones.'"

A big ol' rebellious bulb of a tear leaked out of the corner of Dre's eye.

Janelle gripped Dre's arm. "See there, I'm speaking truth now, aren't I? There's something in there that hurts, and ignoring it isn't helping. You don't have to tell me, but you sure shouldn't keep it from God."

Dre sniffed. "How do you know this stuff?"

A sad-happy laugh rippled from her friend. "Growing up the way I grew up means you grow up pretty fast. The only way I ever knew to deal with any of the junk in my world was to take it to Jesus. Whether it was the attacks from my stepdad or a girl calling me names in the fifth grade. The big, the small, all of it goes straight to Jesus. I worry when I tell my story to others that they're going to see my redeemed hell and think, *My story isn't that, so why would God care? He's too busy with all the Janelle-sized hurts in the world.* Or, maybe in your case, with Paul-sized disasters. That's the opposite of what I want. I want for people—for you—to know from my life that God loves so big that He cares about each little detail. Your hurts matter to God, and belittling them makes less of His great love. Makes less of Him."

With the sleeve of her sweater, Dre wiped the streams of tears running down her face. Driving was definitely the wrong choice for her.

"What I told you about Tom before?"

"That he thought the sun came up to hear him crow?"

"Good grief, I don't even know what that means." Dre sniffed and laughed and shook her head. "But the thing about him being a player. He wasn't always. Tom was shy and quiet and nice. Humble. Honest. Then his senior year, when Paul's rebellion was all coming to a head, Tom sort of...I don't know. He changed. He started dating around a lot." She paused, swallowed. "Sleeping around."

"You know this for a fact?"

Dre nodded.

"Why did he do that?"

"I don't know. Honestly, I don't know why it bothered me so much either. Why it still bothers me."

Dre could feel Janelle studying her. Not with judgment, but it was unnerving nonetheless.

"Yeah, you do," Janelle said.

Heat flooded Dre's face, covering her ears and neck too. She squeezed the steering wheel and sighed. "Yeah. See? Dumb. I'm like the only college-aged virgin left in this country, so it's weird and ridiculous to hope the guy I would maybe fall in love with would have had the same values. Standards. I don't know. Maybe if I hadn't known Tom all through growing up, it'd be different. Maybe if I didn't know the girls he'd slept with, it wouldn't bother me so much. Maybe it's completely unfair of me to have expected him to stay that quiet, honest guy he'd been when we were younger."

From the corner of her eye, Dre could see Janelle tip her head, listening. The dam had been breached, and Dre kept talking. "You know I Googled about this last night—pretending I was working on my project? Typed in *I'm a virgin but...*" She left the rest unsaid. "Do you know how many others must have typed in the same thing? A lot, because there were a ton of hits. Recent. Do you know what the most common response was? *Get over it. It has nothing to do with you, so why do you let it bother you?*"

"Is that Tom's response?"

A shiver rippled in Dre's chest. Tom had basically invited her to say what she felt about his past. Seemed like he wanted her to confront him. She couldn't bring herself to do it—it felt slimy. She shouldn't be holding on to this stuff. Holding him accountable for sins that weren't her business.

"Dre?"

"I don't know. We didn't talk about it much."

"Because he'd be mad? Defensive, maybe?"

No. Very clearly, no.

"Would he tell you to get over it—that it had nothing to do with you, so forget about it?"

Would he? Fear suddenly felt like a vice clamping on her heart. What if he did? Is that really what she was afraid of? Maybe in part. But also, she was mad about it. Mad that he'd done it. And that seemed so shallow of her. Self-righteous and petty. She didn't want him to see that part of her. It was hard enough to admit it to herself.

Dre glanced at Janelle. "What would you do?"

Drawing a breath, Janelle turned her gaze toward the road ahead. "Not sure if you mean if I were you or him. But here's where I sit. Someday, God willing, I'll meet a man who looks at me the way Tom looks at you, and I'm gonna have to be honest about my past. About the ugly things that are in my head, my memories that I wish with all my heart weren't there. Then I'll pray that he'll be able to handle it with grace and strength, remembering that *love keeps no records of wrong*."

"But you didn't do anything wrong, Janelle. That stuff was done *to* you."

"The abuse? Yeah. But trust me, Dre. I've done other stuff that was *my* choice. Chased after wholeness in ways that I knew were wrong. Your Tom and me? We're really not that different. Someday, some man might have to come to terms with my choices—and I promise you, my response to him isn't going to be, 'It didn't involve you, so get over it.'"

A long silence settled in the car while Dre sorted through it all. Tom. Janelle. Their lives and stories. She'd known Janelle had regrets about her own choices. Somehow, though, those choices seemed to be justified for Janelle. She'd lived in a nightmare, so who could blame her for seeking comfort and identity in destructive ways? But Tom?

Love keeps no record of wrongs.

He was repentant. Changed. Yet she was holding him in blame because he didn't have a good excuse like Janelle.

Comparison turned toxic.

What if God treated her that way? He didn't. Doesn't. Because love kept no record of wrongs.

***

Uncertainty gnawed like a toothless dog. Not really painful, but undeniable, and turning Tom a little bit raw. Needing something to do with his hands, his energy, he headed toward the Rustin ranch south of town. The pile of firewood out back of the old farmhouse had looked a little lean. Surely Paul wouldn't mind him imposing some help on the situation.

The supply of sticky buns Tom had picked up from Ms. May's was welcome, and Grams Rustin brewed a fresh pot of coffee to go with them. Gathered around the small round table in the little dining room off the kitchen, Tom settled into a sense a belonging with this group, even if the doubt and anxiety about Dre kept jawing his heart.

"Been nice, having the table full of a pair of fine young men again," Grams said, her hand a little shaky as she poured coffee for the boys. "Jasper, didn't we worry? Heavens, we worried." Her gaze, certainly blurred by the milky white that had been clouding her blue eyes over the past year, fell on Paul.

"Prayed, Helen," Pops said, his voice gravely, but a tenderness in his eyes. Jasper Rustin was tough as nails. All cowboy. Hard work and leather and tough love. Thing about it though—that tough love was *big*, and it pretty much had saved Paul.

Grams laughed. It was weak and a little breathless, but a laugh nonetheless. "All right, old man. You prayed. I worried enough for the both of us. But here you boys are"—her hand landed on Paul's shoulders—"a pair of fine young men. I'm prouder than a hen with her first batch of chicks."

Tom couldn't help a small smile. When he glanced at Paul, he caught the bounce of his friend's Adam's apple and a quick-passing emotion filter through his eyes. Some days had moments inside them that refocused the big picture.

Grace. It really was amazing, and Paul wasn't about to brush that off as nothing. This chance—this undeserved second chance—meant the world to Paul, and Tom knew it. Saw it in the way his friend worked. The way he'd cared for his aging grandparents. And recently, in the way Paul had reconciled with his sister. It had been a little breathtaking.

Love poured out with forgiveness like the kind Grams and Pop had given their grandson was rare and stunning. It had a way of making everyone witness to it want to conform a little bit more to its likeness.

Thomas Kent was the last man to be an exception. As much as he thirsted for grace—from heaven and from one young woman in particular here on earth—he wanted to give it too. Wherever, to whomever—his soul had been lit with a desire to be defined by grace.

Right there, in the warmth of that run-down kitchen, with the smell of strong coffee, Grams's flowery perfume, and Pop's old shaving musk filling the space, and with his best friend sitting beside him getting ready for another day of work, Tom let the resolve cement. No matter what happened—how anything worked or didn't work out with Dre, or with the DNR with whom he'd hoped and prayed for a job, or the farm down in Kansas, or anything else the uncertain future could hold—Tom wanted his life to be defined by God's grace. Like Pop and Grams.

The resolution felt monumental, which seemed somehow a contradiction to the fact that the conversation at the small table moved forward. They ate, drained their coffee, and moved into the day's work. But Tom let the decision captivate his mind, and on the heels of a most sincere and possibly second-most profound prayer of his life—*Jesus, make me more like you*—his thoughts and heart turned back to Dre.

The need to tell her about it pushed upward and hard, and whether she called him that night like he'd asked her to or not, he'd be talking to her. With that, the toothless dog named *uncertainty* gave up, and Tom looked forward to the day.

Though Pop Rustin seemed a little pale, and Tom and Paul were more than capable of handling the task on their own, the old man had pulled on his red-checked hat and corduroy winter work coat. Couldn't let the boys chop wood on their own. No sir. Pop would work until the day he met Jesus face to face. And then he'd probably ask for some kind of tool to get started on whatever the Master wanted him to do up there. Work was a blessing to Jasper Rustin, and he did it well.

Together, the three of them strode to the tree line, Paul and Tom swinging a chainsaw from their right hands, and Pop Rustin with a fistful of orange ties he'd use to mark branches that needed to come out. The leftover shadows of the previous night melted in the strengthening light of the new morning sun.

A new day was on, some good work ahead. Tom dove into it, purpose redefined.

Chapter Sixteen

DRE PALMED HER CELL PHONE IN ONE HAND AND FINGERED THE UNOPENED ENVELOPE IN HER RIGHT.

Sitting on her bed in their dorm, she let the circling thoughts in her head have full rein. It'd been a long drive back, and she was too tired to pull in all the *what-ifs* and *what nows* that turned her head into a mess.

Janelle—as usual—had given her some soul-deep insight. Good stuff to take in, let soak, and allow her heart to grow. Her friend would do well as the counselor she was studying to be—and was suited to lead the college Bible study that met on campus. Dre would do well to listen. And she did. Honest, she did.

But there was also a hard reality when it came to all the emotion that swirled in her heart about Tom. It wasn't only about the past. There was the future to consider, and she'd been listening when he'd talked about loving Rock Creek—the land and the people, and hoping to have a position with the Department of Natural Resources located there. He'd been as passionate about that as she was about Tami Cooper's design class and the possibilities beyond. If they were talking about testing the waters of emotion that clearly existed between Tom and her, then there were some barriers she didn't think they could ignore.

After all, she'd been determined to come back to Texas for a reason.

Was she overthinking this? After all, Tom hadn't been talking about forever. Not yet. Not now. Right? Normal people didn't worry about the distant future like this, did they? It'd be so much easier to just...

Just what? Leap headlong into something that was bound to hurt? That sounded...awful. And stupid. And very much *not* Dre.

But she'd promised him a phone call. She could do that much. Should do that much. Maybe she'd better put an end to all this while she was at it. Clean. Easy.

That seemed right. Lifting the phone and punching in Tom's number, she let a breath sigh from her lungs, telling herself it was relief. She hit Dial and waited for the connection to start ringing, and a sudden curiosity overpowered her. That envelope, still in her left hand, became demanding. With her thumb, she slipped it open, and while holding the phone to her ear with her shoulder, she slipped the folded sheet of lined paper out.

Two lines, penned in Tom's small, no-frills penmanship, scrawled black against white in the middle of the page. Two short lines.

Not what she'd expected.
Dre-
I don't want you to be one of my mistakes either.
I'll do whatever it takes.

Two short lines. That was all it took. Clean and easy? Not a chance. She was undone.

***

Tom wandered from the bathroom, steam rushing from the narrow door behind him. Running a hand over his wet dark-blond hair, he moved to his bedroom to find a sweatshirt to pull on over his white tee.

The white light of his phone caught his attention, and he picked it up off the dresser where he'd left it to charge.

Missed call.

Seriously? He'd been in the shower for all of ten minutes, sure that Dre wouldn't call for at least another hour. Apparently the girls hadn't messed around. Beelined toward the border.

He slipped the charger plug from the port and tapped the Home button to make sure it had been Dre's call he'd missed. Yep. Two minutes before, but she hadn't left a message. Snagging the sweatshirt he'd come for, he ducked into the warmer material while he tapped Call Back on the phone.

It rang. Rang again. By the fifth ring, Tom scowled. Not the mad kind, but the confused sort. She'd just called him, so what—

"Hey." Her voice sounded...forced? Heavy?

Tom tried to block away the sense of falling as he slowly lowered onto the sagging secondhand couch in the living room. "Hi." He swallowed. Great. Awkward. Not what he'd hoped for at all. "How's the drive?"

"Long."

"You got there before I thought you would."

"Yeah, well, Janelle drove the better half of the trip, and for some reason the only cliché she doesn't know or understand is *she has a lead foot.*"

Tom chuckled. Dre...sniffed?

"You okay?" he asked.

"Yeah..." Her sigh whispered over the airwaves. "Tom?"

"Yeah?"

"I read your note."

His gut clenched. Heart spiraled. "Is that...did I make you upset?"

The silence from her end made him sweat. "Dre?"

"I don't know how to do this. With you. Like this."

"Don't know how to—"

"I'm scared."

"Oh." He shoved his fingers into his wet hair. "Of me? That I'm not being sincere?"

"No. But...well, are you?"

"Completely. I wish I knew how to tell you. Or show you." Could he show her from thirteen hours away? How would that look?

"You don't really even know me anymore, Tom."

"Okay." But he did, didn't he? Saw everything he'd liked about her in her words and actions over the past week. She'd changed, sure. Who didn't over four years? She'd grown up. Become more confident. But she smiled the same. Had the same big, wide-open heart. Adorable determination. And unique ability to see potential where others didn't even think to look.

Her sigh cut his thoughts short. "Maybe I'm afraid that I don't know you."

She knew him, didn't she? How could she not know him when they'd practically grown up side by side? Tom squeezed his eyes shut as a wave of defeat washed over him. What now? Let her go?

"Tom?"

He brushed a hand over his face and then made a fist under his chin. "Do you want to know me?" Once the words were out, he felt like he was out on a wire, suspended in space and in the dark. He heard the rustling of paper on the other end, and then her sniff.

"Did you mean what you said at the barn last night?" she asked.

"About honesty?"

"Right."

"I meant it." Was that hope holding him steady? He grabbed

on to enough courage to plunge ahead. "If you want to know me—or anything about what happened before—you have full rein. Ask. I won't lie to you, Dre."

"Even if the questions are hard?"

"Especially when the questions are hard." He drew a breath, fortifying himself for what was sure to come. For the *whys*.

"Okay."

The pause extended again. Tom waited, still expecting the questions. One hard one in particular—the one he'd known had bothered her most. She didn't ask.

"Okay?" he finally said.

"Yes. We could try this...um...what is this, exactly?"

Man, to be a poet right now. Words didn't slide off his tongue. Hadn't ever. Of him and Paul, he'd been the quiet one. The one who usually faded into the background.

But he'd told her to ask him anything. He'd promised no lies.

"This is me telling you that in these last four years, you haven't left my mind." He stood from the couch, hoping it'd give him more confidence. "Me saying that if you were gone another four years, I'd still be missing you."

***

Dre finished her presentation, her ideas captured on the screen at the front of the classroom and samples of wood flooring, a color palate, and complementing fabrics on a board she'd put together before she'd gone back to Rock Creek.

Mrs. Cooper stood to one side of the class, head tilted, arms loosely crossed. "It's a bold choice. Not super trendy right now, but classic. Do you feel you can sell that in a time when the home improvement shows are pushing hard on current trends?"

Dre inhaled, an attempt to smother the nerves that had

made a squall in her stomach. "In the interview with the client, they made a specific request for something that would be enduring. Both calm and clean and able to press through the trends that shift with the calendar. I made careful palate and fabric choices with that specific request in mind."

Face still neutral—or not impressed?—Mrs. Cooper stepped toward Dre. "One might argue that your choices are too neutral. That they will contribute to a sterile, unpersonal feel to the space you're proposing—which would be a problem, as the client also used words like *comfortable*, *homey*, and *welcoming* in their request survey."

She was failing. Heart dropping like an acorn from a high branch, Dre carefully kept her shoulders straight and desperately tried to keep confidence and positivity in her presentation. "I believe that given a soft, neutral background, with a classic feel that is perennial, the client will find that we can incorporate pieces within the space that will achieve the homey, welcoming feel that they're looking for. Greenery, placed strategically, for example. Carefully selected artwork and pictures that have personal meaning and aesthetic beauty. Personal touches placed on a clean canvas can achieve the balance I believe the clients are seeking."

One corner of Mrs. Cooper's mouth quirked as she held a look on Dre. "Class, do we have any other questions or concerns?"

Unnerved, Dre swallowed, fought to maintain an unflappable expression, and scanned her classmates. Though there were only twelve of them, she felt exposed and way too vulnerable as she stood there open to their unfiltered evaluation. A few eyebrows jumped upward—also uncertain.

A girl in the corner scowled with a mild shake of her head. "I think she won't sell this. People always say things like 'I want a clean, uncluttered feel' and then pick out the most unclean, bold color palate, cluttered furniture, and bizarre fabric combinations. I think it's a mistake to take those ambiguous words to heart as you have and ignore the current trends. I feel like you'll lose your clients."

Still unreadable, Mrs. Cooper pivoted to face the critic at the back of the room. "Ah. The ever-present dilemma when dealing with people. Do they mean what they say—or is there something in a subtext somewhere that we need to read? This brings us to an element of the job that is difficult—if not impossible—to teach. The ability to listen, not only to what a person is saying, but what they are meaning. This is tricky. It requires that we get to know our clients—their honest preferences, not just verbalized ideas or trendy whims—so that we can serve them as the unique people they are. Here is one of the more time-consuming elements that many designers skip, and it'll cost them sometimes. Taking the time to really invest in our clients rather than running a meeting with them like a cattle chute."

The digital clock on the wall turned over to 3:00 p.m. and the other students cleared their tables of notebooks and laptops. Dre remained at the front, feeling like a fish on a hook dangling above the water, where she couldn't breathe.

Ms. Cooper dusted her hands together and smiled over the room. "Good discussion and points to think about. We'll do the last three presentations on Wednesday. Until then..." She waved, and in a chorus of screeching stools against linoleum and shuffling of bags, the others left.

Ears ringing and face warm, Dre replaced the clicker remote on the front table and moved to detach the projector cords from her laptop. The room, which was one moment a clutter of footfalls and voices, settled into silence until a pair of heels popped against the floor, the sound behind her and coming near.

"You handle criticism well, Dre." Mrs. Cooper arrived at her side. "I'm curious to know if you'd stick to your initial instinct on this design, or if you'd compromise?"

Dre blinked, wished the heat on her face didn't show, because without a doubt, she knew it did. "I'm not sure I can say. This is a fictional job, and we didn't get to actually interview a real client. All I'm working with is a written paper on what the client said, so it's hard to read their true likes and dislikes in that."

Mrs. Cooper nodded. "Very true." She turned and hopped up onto the front table, legs crossing at the ankles. "If this were a real job, with real people, what would you do?"

Laptop closed, cords coiled neatly, Dre laid her hands on the tabletop and paused for a quiet moment. If the client was her mother, what would she do? Mama liked blue, but had a tendency to overdo it—blue on the walls, the countertop, the backsplash. Blue dishes. Blue linens. It had become a sea of blue that was overwhelming—and not only in Dre's opinion. Mama had asked Dre what she thought she'd do different in her kitchen. There were some structural layout things Dre would change, but the biggest change she'd make would be to give Mama a chance to love blue again by making it special.

But she knew Mama, so that was different.

"I guess it would start with what you said: get to know them. What does their everyday look like? What things do they gravitate to? What comes up in conversation that is obviously important? Maybe that means going to a furniture store together and initially watching what they're drawn to, and then asking why? What do you like about that? Maybe creating a profile of styles and going through that together, watching for what lights them up. What makes them smile or makes their expressions relax. Find a way to find out what speaks to them as an individual."

Finally, a smile widened on Mrs. Cooper's face. Her rings clinked against the stainless steel of the table as she tapped her fingers along the edge. "Of all the things I could teach you about design, the most important really doesn't have anything to do with color palates or fabrics or form or function. When we learn to listen—to *really* listen to people—we will begin to do our jobs well."

Relief rolled through Dre. She lifted a wobbly smile and collected her laptop.

"Remember what I told you before break, Dre?"

Dre paused and looked back at her teacher.

"You have a gift for seeing potential. Not only in buildings and spaces—though that is very clearly evident. But also in people. You will find, I think, that the most rewarding part of any kind of job you take on will be finding a way to bring joy to others. You can do that. I have absolutely no doubt." Mrs. Cooper hopped back to the ground, her heels punching a happy tap-tap onto the floor. "And also, just so you know, I agree with your choices on this project." She winked. "Well done."

Anxiety turned to drifting confetti, and Dre lifted a real smile. "Thanks."

Mrs. Cooper dismissed her with a nod, and Dre wanted to run out of the classroom and call someone who would let her squeal about her success. Funny. The first people who should have come to mind were Mama or Janelle.

Not Tom.

But it was Tom. And it was weird that that didn't feel weird.

Chapter Seventeen

Tom wasn't much for email.

It had seemed a little silly. Call and say watchya gotta say, right? Or mail a letter. Nothing wrong with old school.

That was before.

He'd had things he'd wanted to say last night. Stuff he'd wanted to tell Dre. Hadn't been able to, and though there was a list of reasons why he couldn't on the phone, there wasn't a single reason he could think of not to tell her somehow.

So he'd try this email business, because old school in light of this new development seemed tragically slow.

For a time, he sat and stared at the computer screen, wondering how he'd made it through college having to write so many papers on a blank screen with an infernal blinking cursor. But then he shut his eyes and let the memory of Dre's hesitation drown his fears. She wanted to know if he was sincere...

Dre

I was at your grandparents' yesterday morning. Sitting at their table, I was suddenly overwhelmed by the way that they live. How they love. Paul is different now, so much of that because of how they loved him. Not in the whatever-kind-of-hell-you-want-to-raise-is-fine way, but a hard, strong, unbending kind of way. Probably that doesn't make sense— although, they're your grandparents, so maybe you know exactly what I mean.

*It occurred to me how much I want to be like them. Love
tough like them.*

Tom reread what he'd written. Hardly a romantic letter to a
girl he was desperate to win. But it had been what he'd wanted
to tell her the night before. And it was honest. Maybe that was
a start.

***

Dre didn't have time to make that happy-squeal phone call
she'd had the impulse to make. Her next class had been across
campus, and her visit with Mrs. Cooper meant she had to get
there on a run. But she finished her spreadsheet assignment for
accounting a little early and clicked open her email to kill the
time.

There at the top in bold type was the name *Thomas Kent*,
and her heart did that funny squeeze thing again. She clicked
it, and it opened, and she devoured his short note. Surprised,
because it didn't say anything that she'd expected—maybe
hoped for. But also, in the ordinary, everydayness of what Tom
had shared, she caught a glimpse of his heart.

It kind of melted her.

She clicked Reply and let her fingers take over.

Tom,

*Tough kind of defines my grandparents—in all the best
ways. I want to be like them when I grow up too.*

*You know that presentation I was working on for my design
class? I had to give it today, and at first it seemed like I nailed
it. And then it didn't. But afterward, my professor talked with
me, and now I feel like I did. Nail it, I mean. I wanted to jump
and squeal. And call you.*

Is that weird?

***

Weird? No. My phone is sadly silent. Waiting for you to call, jumping and squealing.

Tom typed out the words and zipped the email off into cyberspace. Maybe he should call her? He picked up his cell but then shoved it into his back pocket. He'd wait, give her a chance to get his email. Later tonight, he'd call. Or in the morning. His stomach had been giving him a hunger fit since he'd walked in the door anyway, lunch at the Rustin ranch apparently a long-gone memory. He set himself to making supper, putting in a big effort to push back thoughts of Dre, of wishing she'd called, and the impulse to dial her up on the spot.

Meat was sizzling on the griddle iron his mom had given him, when his phone buzzed. Slipping it from his pocket, he was actually surprised to see Dre's name lit up on the face. Might be a new favorite moment. A grin played against his mouth while he let a little glee sink in.

"Hey there."

"Hi." She sounded shy and happy all at once, which made his grin spread into a full smile.

"So tell me," he said.

"About my presentation?"

"Yeah. Include the jumping and squealing. I want the full effect."

Her laugh felt like soft fur brushing against his ear, warming his face and heart. When she launched into a full rundown of the class, he flipped the heat off on the griddle and switched the knobs on the stovetop to low. Her replay was animated, and when she got to the part where her teacher—Mrs. Cooper, was it?—told her she'd have made the same choices, a little squeal came from Dre's end of the line.

Tom laughed. "So you crushed it."

"I did. I think. Hope."

"I'm sure you were awesome."

"Yeah, no. I was scared to death, especially when the other student said I'd lose the client. What a thing to say. Can you imagine saying that to someone? In front of a whole class?"

"I can't imagine you saying that to another person. But you're more kind than most."

The other end of the line went still for a breath. Like she wasn't sure what to do with that. Then, "So...what are you doing?"

"Making supper."

"What's for supper?"

"T-bone, baked potato, some corn from the little patch of sweet corn my grandpa planted last year."

"Sounds like a standard cowboy meal. Rustin beef?"

"Of course. Every day."

"That sounds well rounded." Sarcasm colored her voice. "Maybe you need some vegetables that aren't mostly starch in with that menu."

Tom crossed an arm over his chest as he leaned against the counter. "I could go for Dre's tomato soup with a side of molasses drop cookies, but the cook's gone south for the winter."

She chuckled. "Recipes are in Mama's kitchen. You're welcome to go make copies anytime."

"Not the same."

Another lull drifted between them. He wondered if she were there in front of him, if she'd be blushing. Or maybe she'd be bold, the way she'd been in the muddy working pen. Eyes set on his. Mouth drifting nearer...

"Hey, Tom?"

He straightened. Tried not to clear his throat too loudly. "Yeah."

"Thanks for the email."

Suddenly he was all for email. And anything else that came along that would put that kind of smile in her voice.

***

Stopped at the store after work to pick up some non-starchy vegetables. I'm not sure which ones those are, so I got a rainbow. For the record, carrots are good. Broccoli is bad. And I think I should get credit for eating Veggie Straws instead of potato chips. But that's not what I wanted to tell you.

Shelby finally got Chuck to propose—which I'm sure is quite a story all by itself. Not one I'm interested in hearing. But she was gushing about it in aisle three, and saw me. With her cheerleader energy dialed up to full blast, she grabbed my arm and told me that we had to find a way to get you home by June. She wants to have the wedding in the barn.

Look what you've started.

Something soft wrapped around Dre as she read Tom's email. She had a ton of homework to get to, and needed to find something a little more fortifying than the to-go muffin she'd picked up after her last class, but the hope that Tom had written to her again had put everything on pause.

That something soft was him thinking of her. But there was also something a little sharp in the wrap, poking at her as she read about Shelby. She'd envisioned a wedding in the barn. Hadn't been Shelby's.

Dre shook her head, scooted off her bed, where she'd landed to read Tom's note, and searched for protein and non-starchy vegetables. Clearly she needed something good for her to ground her thoughts. Although, Veggie Straws sounded pretty yummy. Her imagination didn't take the hint she was trying to feed it though. Those images in her head were still of the barn. In June. Maybe a bouquet of lilacs. And a good-looking man whose steel-blue gaze might could make her rethink Texas.

Holy hay bales. To borrow something from Janelle's well-stocked arsenal, she was a few pickles short of a barrel.

And yet, she smiled. Kept right on dreaming, never once remembering all her curated reasons to guard her heart.

*****

The first weeks of December slipped by, full of checking cattle, breaking ice, cleaning out the barn, maintaining the pile of firewood, or whatever else Pop Rustin put them up to, and coming home good and tired. But the best part of Tom's days were the mornings, when, with coffee nearby, he'd write a new email knowing he'd come home to find one from her. And later in the evenings, they'd talk. Some phone calls were short—Dre had a lot of homework, or she'd be heading off for a late shift at work.

Other conversations were long.

They talked about everything and nothing, and in the almost three weeks since she'd finally come home for a visit, Tom had gone from missing her like crazy and wondering what she was doing to knowing what she was doing and missing her even more. This thing between them had moved a little bit like a landslide, which surprised him. Not on his part—that wasn't the surprise. But hers. Maybe that was in his head though. Something he'd convinced himself of because hope had a way of putting blinders on in some cases.

Snow flew in a brisk wind outside when Dre called. Tom was working on the last of his heated-up canned chicken noodle soup with a side of raw carrots—just to make Dre smile—when her call buzzed. He wiped his mouth and calmed the leaping that bounced inside his chest, which was a normal reaction whenever he saw her name lit up on his phone. But tonight he'd hoped to talk about a few things that made him a little anxious.

She sounded tired. A little stressed. Finals were looming, and she had a lot of tests to study for. But her voice soothed as they talked. He told her about the sunrise that morning, how the coming snowstorm had darkened the northern part of the sky, but the southern half had seemed even more determined to give a royal entrance to the coming day.

Dre loved the sunrise as much as she did the sunset—

something she'd told him in an email last week. She also loved Christmas, a fact he remembered from their growing-up years.

"Are you coming home on your break?" he asked, hope tight in his chest. He couldn't believe how badly he ached to see her. She'd only been gone for three weeks. How on earth had he gone over four years without a glimpse of her wide smile, warm eyes, beg-him-to-touch hair?

Her long sigh had his heart plummeting. "I can't, since I took the whole week of Thanksgiving off. I have to work Christmas."

"Really? But you're a student."

"Yeah, I know, and I could probably toss that out and get some sympathy. But the thing is, my scholarships only cover fifteen credit hours next semester, and I'm taking nineteen. I need to work. There's no way around it."

"You're taking nineteen hours?" Good grief, that was a heavy load.

"Right. So I can graduate in May."

"And you're working?"

"Gotta pay the bills."

"Dre, how are you doing all of this and not collapsing?"

"I'm fine." Her warm voice softened. "It fills the time, you know? And Pop always told us we were built for work."

Pop did say that, even to this day. But still, that was a lot to take on. Also, it meant that she wasn't coming home.

"What if I came down there?" As soon as the words were out, Tom held his breath. It was one of those *define the relationship* moments. He knew where he stood on the matter, and thought he probably knew where she was too. But still...

Her pause lasted a little too long.

"Dre?"

"I'm here. Just...thinking."

"Are you freaking out?"

"No. Not really freaking. But."

A sharp jab cut into his chest. Tom forked his fingers into his hair while his thoughts swirled. How had he misjudged this? Everything seemed good. She was open with him—to him. Their conversations were easy.

Man, he missed her.

"Tom?"

"Right here, Dre. Waiting for you."

"Don't be...mad. Please?"

"I'm not mad. Confused. Maybe a little frustrated. Just...explain this to me."

He heard her sniff. "I feel like this is going really well."

"Okay..."

"I like where we are right now."

"I'm not sure what that means, Dre. Where are we?"

Silence.

What did that mean? Was she seeing other guys? Was this a casual thing for her—like a pen pal? Like he was her good buddy up north she could share the details of her days with, laugh with, joke with, but that was it?

Had he not been clear with how he felt about her? How could she not get this?

Yeah, actually, he was angry. He didn't even try to weed it out of his voice. "Look, maybe things are different in your world, Dre. But let me be clear. I miss you. There's a high probability that I'm in love with you. If this is a casual thing on your end, I need you to be straight with me."

"It all feels really fast to me, Tom. That's all."

"What does that mean then?"

"Can we keep things where they are? For now?"

"You mean distant? Emails and phones calls, but keep a good thirteen hours apart at all times?"

"Tom." Her voice broke.

Tom slid his eyes shut, rolled a fist into his hair. His heart pulsed hard and hot, but hearing her cry doused a lot of the anger.

"I'm sorry," she whispered.

And the rest of the flames died. He uncurled his fingers and finger combed his hair back into place. "Don't cry, Dre. I'm sorry."

Her stuttered breath whispered over the line. Finally, she said, "I do miss you."

Confusion swam with misery. She missed him but didn't want him to visit. Made perfect sense. What was he supposed to do now?

Table it. He guessed. What else was there? "You sound tired, Dre. Maybe I should let you go."

"I guess." Her sigh sagged, pulling his heart until it felt like it would tear. "I've got some more studying to do."

An awkward goodbye, and the call ended. The rest of the night, Tom spent restless and frustrated, the constant talk of ESPN's *NFL Matchup* a background to the debates launching in his mind.

The loudest of which? He'd told her he was in love with her. Out loud. She hadn't touched that. So where did that leave him?

Chapter Eighteen

"It's like you're bent on hugging a riled porcupine." Janelle spoke from across the table they shared in the community cafeteria. "Why are you doing this to yourself?"

Dre dropped her head against the table and pounded. "I. Don't. Know." She sat back up and looked at Janelle, misery oozing through her.

"He offered to come here," Janelle said. "For Christmas. Are you insane?"

"No. Some." She slid both hands into her hair and gathered the length of it into a tight ponytail. "I froze. Or something. I don't even know. I kept thinking, *He'll come here and that'll be it. I'll drop out of school, forget all my plans, and ride off into the sunset with him only to resent that I didn't get my degree and he stole my dreams.*"

"That would be awful." Janelle raised her eyebrows. "Really think that's how it'd play out?"

Dre's forehead landed on the table again. "No. Maybe? Doesn't really seem like him, does it?"

"The guy who pulled off a political miracle to make sure you got the chance to do your barn thing? No. Doesn't seem like him at all."

"I know. But he's done other things that surprised me. In a bad way."

"Ah."

Dre sat up, jolted by that tone. Head cocked, Janelle crossed her arms. "There it is. The real rub. Girl. I think you're loading the wrong wagon."

"I swear, you start talking, and the more you get going, the more I need an interpreter."

"You haven't talked to him about it, have you?"

Heat filtered onto Dre's cheeks, and she wanted desperately to deny knowing what Janelle was referring to. But that would be childish, and she was really trying to not be childish. Even if her lingering issues beneath the fear of regret seemed fairly childish.

A long sigh dragged from Dre's lung. "No."

Janelle nodded, and in a weird twist of unexpected personality quirks, didn't say anything.

"I'm being a coward, right?" Dre tried to summon half a grin. "How would you say that?"

"You're crawlin' around like a yaller dog. But that's not me talking right now." Janelle stood, came around the table, and hugged Dre's shoulders. "It's not me in this thing. It's you and Tom. I could sit here and tell you what to do, but it's really not my bucket to fill. You have to decide if giving him the chance to be better than he was is worth the risk."

Dre let that spin in her mind for a while. Long after the girls had called it a night, she lay in her twin dorm-issued bed and wondered if she could be brave enough to tell Tom about her real fears. Both of them—that she resented the choices he'd made in high school and was afraid she'd never get past it, though she knew that kind of made her a jerk. And she felt divided about what a serious relationship with him would do to her plans.

How would he respond to those, if she was honest? She didn't want to feel more stupid. She already felt small about the notch of hurt in her heart she'd been harboring. It'd be so much easier if God would make it go away without involving Tom in the battle.

What do You think about all this?

The prayer found center stage as she squeezed her eyes shut. In three weeks, this was the first she'd checked with God on His thoughts regarding Tom Kent. She'd thought to check with Him, but hadn't done it, for reasons that might truly make her *yaller dog*-ish. Because the deal was, for as outgoing and ambitious as Dre was, she wasn't confrontational, and if her suspicions were true—God wanted her to be honest with herself and Tom—it'd be so very uncomfortable.

With that revelation clear in her mind, Dre had parted company with Janelle. Throughout her evening at work, mind and legs busy waitressing, a whisper turned in her heart. *Be brave.*

The next morning, the email waiting for her from Tom gave her the courage she needed.

***

Couldn't sleep last night. Don't take this wrong—I'm not trying to push my way where you don't want me. But I feel like there are things you don't want to tell me. Dre, just tell me. Please?

***

I didn't sleep well either.

I don't want to push you away. That's not what's happening.

You're right. There are a few things I don't really want to talk about—but it's not about other people or anything like that. But I'm scared to say anything. I'd rather just be happy. It'd be easier to stick to our fun emails and light, easy phone calls that leave me with a smile.

But I guess that wouldn't be the sum of everything between us, would it? Not if we were honest.

I don't like arguments. I hated the conflict between Paul and

*me those last years of school. Honestly, I left because I couldn't
do it anymore. I wanted peace. Now, I really don't want
friction between you and me. So I was trying to figure it out
and deal with it on my own.*

It hasn't been working. So here it is.

*Why did you do what you did your senior year? You were
such a nice guy. Reliable. Honestly good. And then... Are the
stories true?*

*And why did you pick my most vulnerable moment to kiss
me? What did you mean by it?*

Why do I even care about this stuff? It's years in the past...

*I'm sorry, Tom. Clearly I'm not grown up enough for a
grown-up relationship.*

***

A contradiction of emotions collided as Tom read Dre's
email. Relief, because finally, she was willing to talk for real.
Shame, because though he'd been fairly sure about some of the
things that were bothering her, reading them literally put the
past right in his face, and he didn't like it. And then, some
confusion. He'd thought he'd known why she slapped him that
night by the pond. Apparently he hadn't completely
understood.

Sitting at his tiny table alone in the cold darkness of a
winter's night, he reread her words for the twentieth time at
least. The established rhythm of this long-distance
relationship he wanted so much to work had determined that
there would be a phone call within the next hour or so. Things
felt different that night though. Not that he didn't want to
call her, hear her animated voice as she shared her day. It was
that now, finally, she was being honest. Sometimes that was
easier done in black and white.

Dre,

*Just to be up front, I adore you. Hopefully you've got that loud
and clear. I asked you to tell me, so don't you dare feel bad
about talking to me about it.*

Why did I start dating around so much my senior year? The easy answer is that for a while, it was fun. Hanging out with Paul had become stressful and frustrating, and having a date gave me a good excuse to not bear witness to his ever-growing disaster. Spineless, I know, and it left you alone to deal with him, and I'm sorry. Also, finding out that girls liked me was...I don't know. Made me feel good, I guess. There's something in me that longs to know I matter. That for someone, I'm not runner up. I was always the sidekick, you know? The quiet one in the corner. Paul was center stage, and that was fine, but suddenly he wasn't the only one the girls noticed. I guess I got caught up in the headiness of it.

Are the stories true? I don't fully know what was said in the girls' locker room or passed around the halls. Some, yeah, I knew about, and it kind of made me sick. So here's the truth: I slept with Abigail. More than once. I can't even tell you why for sure. Maybe because I was eighteen? Pathetic, I know. A kiss turned into more, and I didn't stop. I also didn't know she'd go around telling everyone and anyone all about it. Didn't know that her stories would breed new tales. I wished then that I hadn't slept with her. I wish now that I hadn't. I'm sorry.

Why did I kiss you?

Not for the reasons you thought.

That kiss was a full year, at least, of me fighting attraction to you because you were Paul's little sister and I wasn't brave enough to deal with however he would have reacted to me liking you. It was me, knowing how much you hurt, and hurting for you, wishing I could make it better. It was me wishing I'd been what you needed that whole year instead of off chasing stuff that ended up making me feel worse.

It was not me messing with you in a vulnerable moment.

I thought you slapped me because of the rumors—because you were disappointed in me. Easy to assume, because I was ashamed of myself. I didn't know you thought I was trying to take advantage...

Never, Dre.

You care because I hurt you. How could I hold that against you? I don't. But I hope that you'll forgive me. If you can't...

I'll accept that. I can't boss you into forgiving me—especially when I know I don't deserve it—and I wouldn't want to even if

I could. But you and me? I can't see us going forward if you can't forgive me. That's not an ultimatum, Dre. Just what's real.

For the record, it kind of kills me to face it.

***

Dre wiped the tears from her cheeks. Tom's words pierced, but somehow in a good way. Like lancing a skin infection, the yuck broke away. Lifting her face to the blue sky above, she breathed in cool air as she soaked in the warm sunshine. *What do You think of all this?*

Peace wrapped her, as beautiful and comforting as that warm Texas sun.

Be brave?

Yes. That whisper was still there. A thread of softness and encouragement. With a long, cool breath, she resettled her laptop and willed courage and honesty into her words.

Girls always think that we own all the insecurity and boys don't even know what it looks like. Why is that?

I forgive you. I'm trying to, at least. I don't know why it's so hard, Tom. None of what you did directly involved me, so I don't know why it's the issue it is with me.

Since we're being honest, you should know that you never stood in Paul's shadow to me. I kind of thought you were the best thing in Rock Creek from the time boys became more interesting than gross in my world. And for the record, I'm a little dazed that you like me—the nerdy, freckle-faced little girl you've seen fall in the mud on multiple occasions.

I landed the top spot in my design class, which means next semester, when we take on a real project under Tami's supervision, I'll have the lead. I'm thrilled and terrified. This is all that's been in my head for the last two years, after I accidently discovered that design flowed in my veins.

Now there's you, and I'm wondering what I'm chasing. It feels a little bit like a crisis.

***

Chase your dreams, Dre. I'm not getting in the way. The last thing I want to be to you is a crisis.
I'm proud of you.
Also, mud, sunshine, snow, rain...doesn't matter. I just see you.

***

Christmas approached. Tom made plans to go to Kansas. The day passed with his family on his grandparents' farm, a quiet settled-ness holding him steady. He'd rather have been with Dre. But they'd found a deeper intimacy because of the conflict the holiday had provoked. It made missing her sweeter, strange as that was. His prayers about her—about them—had turned from a begging *Please, God, let her be mine*, to *Please, show me what would be for her best*. That felt a little more like love. Like the kind of love he'd witnessed in Pop and Grams Rustin.

Their frequent emails continued, not all as deep as those they'd exchanged before Christmas, but every one of them honest. She'd called him on Christmas day, and when she said she missed him, her voice broke in a way that claimed a truth more than her words.

He called her when he made it back to Rock Creek two days later, and after she vented to him about a customer who had spent two hours at one of her tables, ordering what amounted to a five-course meal, and then left her a one-dollar bill as a tip, he battled anger against this faceless jerk who had stiffed the love of his life. The impulse to tell her—not the anger part—the part about him loving her, bulged hard and strong. He caged it. Barely.

He had told her once before; she still hadn't touched it. To say it again, well, it wasn't the risk of another silent rejection. It was the risk that he'd pressure her into something she didn't mean.

That was not what he wanted at all.

Chapter Nineteen

HOMESICKNESS WAS A STRANGE THING.

It was a little like the flu, in that in general, there was a predictable season for it. The newscasters, working off information they gleaned from the Center for Disease Control, would predictably proclaim that "Flu season is coming. Doctors are recommending vaccinations..." This happened every year, and then the season would end and everyone would forget about the flu until the next season.

But there were always outliers. Cases that didn't hit when the season had been declared *open*. Often these little rogue buggers would be the most brutal. They'd slam their victims to a bed and hold them there tight with their evil attacks.

The predictable season for a homesick attack was round about the second month in, freshman year. For Dre, homesickness hit off season. And it slammed her in a way that felt like a rogue flu outlier, attacking her emotions. Flaying them clean inside out and leaving her desperate for relief.

Freshman year, she'd embraced the new life that school, and the geography that had come with it, had offered. She'd missed Mama and Daddy, yes. Even Paul—though her missing him had been tainted with an instinctual guard to not think about it at all lest she wonder where he'd landed himself and why. And Tom—she'd refused to think about him, for a similar instinctual reason. But homesick? Nope. Hadn't been that. Not in the *I'm miserable and can't think about anything else* sort of way.

That second week of January in what was her senior year, a real fit of homesickness hit Dre square in the heart. Miserable was a mild description of the yearning, ache, and obsession she'd developed for her childhood hometown. Rock Creek became the focal place in her mind, and one man who still resided there became the spotlight character.

"Dre, you look like you were sent for and couldn't go," Janelle had said one bright afternoon when their paths crossed at the dorm. "I'd say you done got bit."

Despite her heart full of longing, Dre chuckled. "Bit by what?"

"Bit by what." Janelle snorted and rolled her eyes, shaking Dre's shoulders. "As if you didn't know. There's only one bug that bites until a girl's both happy and sad and all she can think about is going home, when before she was begging her roommate to keep her here."

"Talking to you is a little bit like riding a merry-go-round. Do you know that?"

Janelle's smile stretched proud. "Just giving you something to smile about. You love me for it."

"You know I do."

Done got bit. Wonder what Tom would say to that. If he could decipher it at all. She played that conversation out in her mind...

"Janelle says I done got bit," she'd say.

He'd pause to think about it, because Tom rarely said anything he hadn't thought about first. "What bit you?" he'd ask.

Feeling playful and looking for banter, she'd say, "Starts with L and rhymes with dove."

He'd grin. It'd be the sexy, you're mine kind of grin, and her heart would do a delicious dip and roll. And then...

There was that *and* from before. The one she'd fought

against in the pasture the day they'd worked cattle at the river property. Such a flighty fool she'd been. This time she'd step into that *and*, and it'd be the kind that would like to steal her breath and keep her going all at once.

Face warm—well, flaming—Dre breathed a prayer of thanksgiving that Janelle had scurried herself off to class. She also slid rational thinking into place. Clearly she couldn't have that conversation over the phone. She'd miss that look on Tom's face, not to mention that staggering *and*. She'd not miss that.

Pulling her phone out, she tapped until she opened up her calendar. Spring break wasn't too terribly far away. Close enough that she could hold herself together long enough to make it. She'd invite Janelle, because it was a long drive to make by herself, and Janelle had said she'd really liked Rock Creek and staying with Dre's family. When every other co-ed she knew would be heading off to a sunny beach or a ski slope somewhere, she and Janelle would make their way back to Nebraska. Find themselves in the good life. And she'd tell Tom face to face.

Dre sighed. Out loud. The dreamy, lovesick, ridiculous kind of sigh. It made her giggle.

Seemed she'd found the cure for homesickness.

The phone in her hand buzzed. Perfect timing. She couldn't wait to tell Tom.

Except the name on the caller ID wasn't Tom. It was Paul. And the moment she said hello and he answered with a slow, low, "Hey, sis," all her happy thoughts vanished.

"It's Pop." Paul didn't mess around with little niceties. "He had a heart attack this morning while we were out breaking ice." In the pause Paul took to draw a new, shuddering breath, Dre's heart plummeted toward her shoes. "Dre, he's not coming home."

***

Tom sat in the cab of his pickup outside the Rustins' house in town. Dre should be in there with her family, letting the tears of grief roll right alongside her mama's. She needed to be home. There were moments over the past few weeks that he'd felt stuck in what to do when it came to Dre. She was sorting through some things, and he couldn't do it for her. The fix-things guy in him fought like a drowning man against that, but there wasn't anything he could do more than keep being honest and keep talking, whether it be by phone call or email.

But this crisis? This one he could put action into, and that was a relief.

He scrolled to her name in his contacts, which was to say that he hit the second one that came up on favorites—the first being voicemail—and dialed. Her voice was weepy and strained when she answered on the second ring. "Tom?"

"Hey, sweetheart. You okay?"

"No." And then she was quiet-sobbing. He could tell by the closely timed sniffles. "My Pop died…"

"I know." His heart hurt, and tears stung the back of his eyes while he wished he were there with her. "I'm so sorry."

She continued to cry, and for a minute, that was all there was between them. It was achy, but somehow comfortable too.

"I need to come home," she said, her words broken and breathless.

"Listen, you go ahead and cry, and know I wish I was there to hold you. But also know that I'm heading home right now to find a way to get you here as soon as possible. Okay?"

"But—"

"Dre, let me do this. Please?" He curled a grip on the steering wheel. "I need to do something. Let me get to my computer and I'll get you a flight."

"I can't afford that."

"That's not what I said. You're not paying for it."

"Tom." His name on her breath sounded like argument and longing all at once.

"Please, Dre. Let me help."

She sniffed again, and after another shuddered sigh, she whispered, "Okay."

***

Tom had called her back within an hour, and Dre let relief override the worry at his help. Truth was, it was nice to have someone take care of her. She'd been doing that job pretty much solo for the past four years, and while she'd dabbled in a little bit of pride over the fact that she could and did handle life on her own, having Tom step into the middle of her grief and handle some of the practicalities was a relief.

He'd laid out the options, wanting to know which airport she wanted to fly from and refusing to tell her price differences. She could have looked them up herself, but... What if it hurt his feelings for her to be so obstinate in her independence? Would it? Did it matter if it did?

In this, she decided that it would matter, and she'd let him take care of it. All of it. So he set her up on an early flight the next morning, told her he'd be at Denver International when she landed and would get her home to her mama.

All she could say was thank you—and it felt a little bit like a soft bear hug to have him simply say "you're welcome" and know he really would see to all the other details.

She arranged to miss classes, figured out a ride to the airport, and packed her bags. When Janelle dropped her off the next morning, Dre boarded her first plane ever in her life, by herself.

Before the flight even levelled off for cruising, Dre knew the two hours ahead of her were going to be long and a little bit awful. Her stomach rolled as her equilibrium wigged out. By the time they made a rocky touchdown in Denver, everything in Dre wanted to curl up in a dark place, cover her head, and sob. And throw up.

Which she did—the vomiting part—but she made it into the terminal bathroom first. Puking didn't settle her stomach much, so when she met Tom at the passenger pickup door, she still felt like a wrung-out rag.

"Uh-oh." He jogged the remaining space between them, took the handle of her pull-along bag she'd borrowed from Janelle, and lifted the strap of her backpack from her shoulder. "Bad flight?"

"I don't know. It was my first, so I have nothing to compare it to."

He pulled her into his chest, and she sagged against him, only slightly appalled that she hadn't any gum and probably smelled like puke, but mostly too miserable to care overly much.

"My mom gets airsick all the time, and for some reason orange juice followed by mint gum settles her when she lands," Tom said. "Want to try some?"

"That sounds like a very weird combination. But I'm desperate."

He chuckled and brushed a kiss on her clammy forehead. "There's a drive-thru past the airport grounds. Think you can make it that far?"

"Better than curling up in the parking garage."

A protective arm anchored around her, he turned and guided her toward a vehicle, dragging her one suitcase behind them. When he tapped the fob in his hand and a trunk popped on a passenger car in front of them, Dre paused.

"What's this?"

"Your mom insisted. Said it'd get twice the mileage than my pickup. Also tried to shove a couple of twenties in my palm last night. That I refused."

Dre managed a breathy laugh and turned to press her face back into the solid comfort of his chest. Tears she had refused during the flight and in the public bathroom inside the airport leaked as if they were from a spring melt. Tears for her grandpa. For the stress of this new adventure gone awry. Of relief to know her mama—and this man holding her—were there taking care of her even from Nebraska.

Tom let go of the suitcase handle and wrapped her with both arms. One hand cradled her head, and he curled around her as if to shield her. "Oh, Dre. I'm so sorry."

She fisted the thick fabric of his coat at his sides and let herself be held.

And cried.

Chapter Twenty

Dre dozed, her color better after she'd sipped some OJ and popped a piece of mint Ice Cube gum between her teeth.

Tom cruised the toll highway toward I-76, glancing at her now and then. Even a little green, she'd been the prettiest thing he could remember seeing as she'd walked through those airport doors.

Now, his heart felt like a lasso yanked it hard when her blue eyes fluttered open and landed on him. A faint smile brushed her pretty mouth.

Tom reached for her hand. "Better?"

"Much. Thank you." She straightened from her snuggled position against the seat and blew out a breath. "Boy, if that's normal air travel, count me out. Not. Fun."

But he'd put her back on a plane in less than a week. Tom pushed the thought away.

"Are you hungry now? There's a Chick-fil-A coming up, I think," he said.

"Oh, that's sounds good. Although, you eat chicken?"

Tom snorted. "Yeah, I eat chicken. Why wouldn't I eat chicken?"

Dre chuckled. "Pop. Daddy. Paul. They're not chicken eaters. I guess I thought all men believed chicken was women's food."

"That is weird. And sad for them."

Tom merged onto the interstate, and the exit for the fast-food joint came up fast. He let go of her hand to steer through the turns and then parked across from the front door. Dre shuffled through her pack, tugging out her wallet.

"You're not buying," Tom said.

"You bought my orange juice. And plane ticket."

"And brunch." He motioned toward the restaurant.

With amused challenge, Dre held his gaze, tipping her head to one side. "So it's kind of like a date?"

"Sure. Have we had one of those yet?"

"In the same state?"

Tom laughed. "Phone calls don't count as dates."

"Oh."

Her fallen tone argued otherwise. "Do they?" he asked.

"Well..."

"So how many dates have we had in separate states?"

"I could count on my phone log," she said.

Her grin widened, making the blue of her eyes dance. Tom chuckled as she shifted to leave the car, her wallet in hand.

"Dre."

She shook her head, holding up the wallet. "I don't want to leave it in the car, Mr. Bossy."

He caught her hand in a gentle hold, and she paused, other hand on the door. The sassy grin melted as he stared, and curiosity made the laughter in her eyes fade.

Tom wasn't sure how many heartbeats throbbed between them. How long he'd lost himself there.

"Can I kiss you?" The question, unthought and yet felt deeply, fell from his breath in a whisper.

She softened—her face, her mouth, her posture. Hand slipping from the door handle, she closed the space separating them. He met her mouth, and a thrill pulsed through his chest. Breath caught, he stalled for a moment, then slid his palm against her cheek, angling her mouth for a deeper taste. She was minty and salty, a hint of orange, and entirely addictive. She moved into him, answering his kisses. Her warm palm slid against his chest, over his shoulder, down his arm, sending a crackle of electricity over his skin.

There was the pound of his heart, the pulse of her breath warm against his mouth, and...

Her stomach growled. Dre smiled against his mouth before their lips parted.

"Time's up then?" he whispered.

"You did promise brunch." She nipped his lower lip. "And for the record, this is definitely not our first date. I wouldn't kiss you like that on a first date."

Tom leaned back and laughed. "What was that thing that happened in the working pen over Thanksgiving?"

Pink filtered in her cheeks. "That was..." Her mouth scrunched to one side, making the most adorable *I'm thinking* expression.

"An exception." He cupped her chin, kissed her forehead, her nose, and then pecked her mouth. "Let's go eat."

***

The LORD bless you and keep you...

Pastor Hurst continued the benediction to the end as the gathering at the graveside huddled close. Somehow it seemed appropriate that Pop's service was bitter cold. The man had been tough. Not unloving, but strong. Strong in his work, strong in his opinions, and strong in love.

Dre tipped her chin upward as she walked beside Tom. The green canopy that had offered a little shelter to the family gave way to a white-gray sky, and flakes of cold fluff drifted toward the earth. As a few landed on her cheeks and nose, they melted into tiny puddles, mingling with the tears that silently streamed. Snow was appropriate too. She stopped and faced skyward, letting more flakes kiss her face.

Tom's arm slipped around her. "You okay?"

Dre nodded, inhaled deep. "I'm glad it snowed today." She glanced at him and then looked back to the sky. "The beauty in the hard. As if God was speaking His eulogy for Pop." A sad smile quivered her mouth.

He leaned his forehead against her hair. "You amaze me, Andrea Rustin. Have I told you that?"

She shut her eyes, and another pair of tears leaked onto her cheeks. "Why?"

"The way you see life. How you manage to find beauty everywhere."

The compliment warmed her and attached her heart a little bit more to this man at her side. She leaned into him as they made their way toward Paul's pickup.

They would beat her brother to his vehicle because Paul had stayed with Grams at the graveside. Stopping beside the pickup, Dre looked back toward the casket. Paul stood at Grams's side, steady hand on her back, his size dwarfing her already slight frame. Pop would be proud of him—must have been proud.

Paul had become the man Pop and Grams had prayed for. Over the past days, watching her brother care for Grams, overseeing some of the details that came fast and hard with death, and walking steadily with her through it while managing the work that still needed done at the ranch, any reservations Dre had about who Paul was now vanished. Who he was, was standing right there, strong and loving, just like Pop.

Her brother had come back. Come home.

It's time to come back too.

Dre startled a little, the thought so clear she almost thought the words had come from Tom. But when she glanced up at him, she found he was also watching Paul and Grams.

A needle of unsettledness wove through her. She had her life figured out. Goals and plans that she was working toward—

and being successful at. They weren't here. Rock Creek hadn't been home in four years, and she hadn't foreseen it becoming home again.

Yet when she moved her thoughts toward tomorrow, the day Tom would drive her back to the airport and she'd hitch a plane south, the feeling of homesickness flooded through her. Because she'd miss Tom?

Yes. That had to be it. And Tom was in Rock Creek. But Texas was big, and he'd never been there. Who knew but that he might love it?

Everything could work out. Even if she continued to feel unsettled.

***

The farmhouse was dimly lit when Dre pulled up, but the kitchen window burned yellow against the cold dark night. Paul would still be up.

She parked Tom's pickup. He'd insisted she take it on the fifteen miles of dirt roads between her grandparents' ranch and town. After shutting off the engine, she inhaled, a gentle grin smoothing against her mouth. Tom had been, well, perfect. Not that he was perfect—she knew he wasn't. But over the four days of stress and grief, he'd been her rock. Solid, but not overbearing.

If ever she needed it, that evening was proof. She'd told him she wanted to go visit with Paul before she left the next day. He'd handed her the keys to his pickup because the snow was piling up, kissed the spot near her right eyebrow, and said, "Drive safe. I'll see you in the morning."

Being with him was like being herself in the best possible way. Not fighting for her own identity, and not wondering if she'd be all alone because she was herself. Past failed dating experiences told her how special that security and freedom was, and more and more of her heart clung to it.

She was so falling for Tom. Sitting there in his pickup, remembering his honesty and kindness the past weeks, the way he stepped in beside her without running her over, and...and the feel of his kisses that made her think floating through life might be possible, Dre owned the truth of it.

The unsettled undercurrents of practical details aside, she loved him, and every part of her wanted it to be forever.

She didn't have the emotion or mental capacity to sift through the implications of that, or to figure out those shifty details of a long-distance relationship at the moment though. In that moment, she had a chance to go be with her older brother. Paul had reached out to her several times over. It was time she reached toward him.

So, God, here I am. I'm trying to listen more, you know? Really, I want what You want. Help me to see Paul as he is now.

Filled with a fresh sense of direction—from a peace that poured in her, and from Tom's silent approval of this little trip to the farm—Dre popped the door open. Her boots smacked against the frozen dirt drive, and she strode toward the house.

Paul met her at the kitchen door. "Tom called. Said you were coming. I've got coffee."

"Ah, so you've been given fair warning."

He stepped back as she swept through the door. "He was worried about you. Think he kind of has a thing for you." He winked.

"Hmm." Dre shrugged out of her winter coat and hung it over the back of a kitchen chair. "How's Grams?"

She and her mother had spent the day before the funeral working on freezer meals to stock at the ranch. Just Paul and Grams out at the farmhouse now, and Dre was so thankful he was there. Right where they all needed him to be. Being the man they needed him to be.

"She's exhausted. Went to bed about an hour ago." Paul

poured two mugs with what Dre hoped was decaf and set them on the table. When he moved to sit, she followed. He sighed, ran a hand over his cropped hair. "Can you imagine, Dre? She and Pop were together for sixty years. Sixty. Years."

Could she imagine? More and more, yeah...

"Now he's gone," Paul continued. "I don't know, sis. Grams is solid, but at the same time..." His voice trailed off, and he looked down the hall in the direction of the room their grandparents had shared for so very long.

"You think she'll follow him soon?"

Paul's mouth quirked, a cloud of emotion sheening his eyes. "Guess I wouldn't be surprised." He blinked then, the emotion of it overtaking him. "They're kind of like salt and pepper. Can't split the pair." He inhaled deep and long. "What would I be without them?"

His focus came back to her. "Seriously, Dre. I was such a freaking disaster. But they didn't quit on me, you know? Pop came out to Omaha, told me if I got my GED, I could come work for him. I thought it would be the best deal of my options, which weren't many and looking worse by the moment, so I said yes. Had this picture in my head of me staying upstairs in the room they'd given us as kids. You know? Farm breakfast, a few chores here and there, and farm supper. Top that off with some ranch-hand pay? Yeah. I signed up for that."

His cheeks puffed with air, and then he exhaled, making an explosion sound. "I was in for an awakening."

"I'll bet." She chuckled.

"Yeah, you know it. Some say God loves you too much to leave you where you are, right?"

Dre nodded.

"Apparently Pop did too." A chuckle moved his chest. "Put me out in the bunkhouse. Know how cold it gets out there in winter?"

This time, she shook her head. The *bunkhouse* was a generous title for the small trailer permanently set out in the wind row of pines on the north side of the farmhouse. The only time she or Paul had ever stayed in it was for a fun overnight campout experience in the summer. Back then, staying in it had seemed like an adventure. But actually living in the tin can? Yikes.

"Cold." Paul shivered. "And I developed a keen appreciation for indoor plumbing right quick."

"Oh no. I forgot about the no-plumbing part out there."

"It gets better. In order to keep the heat on, I had to actually *earn* the privilege. Can you imagine?"

Dre looked to the table, a smile poking one side of her mouth. Yeah, she could imagine. "Sounds like Pop."

Paul laughed. "It does, doesn't it? Except somehow it surprised me. Some kind of knothead, right? I was so ready to get out of here, but I didn't have any money and nowhere to go. Who was going to hire a high school dropout who had a record and no references?"

"Well..."

"No one great, that's who. I was stuck. Mad. And pretty much alone, because my good buddy Tom was away at college, as was my sister, and my other friends who'd loved finding ways to get into trouble with me didn't seem to think dirt poor without a future was so awesome anymore."

Dre's smile faded, and tears that were easily surfaced these days burned. She couldn't look at him. But he reached across the table between them and gripped her hand.

"Turns out, it was exactly what I needed." His grip tightened, and Dre looked up. Sincerity like she'd never seen in him brimmed in Paul's eyes. "Don't you dare feel bad for that lonely punk, Dre. Not for a moment. Some of us have to find the bottom of a rock before we realize we have to look up. Know what's amazing though? I could still look up. I should have been buried in all my crap and not able to see anything, but there in my sight was Pop and Grams, holding out their brand of tough love, waiting for me to grab on."

A tear dropped against her nose, and Dre sniffed. "And you did."

"Yeah. In my first real season of sleepless nights and constant work Pop and Grams call *calving*, the hard places in me shifted. My vision cleared, my life came into focus, and the things I was fighting didn't make sense anymore. But my life did. My future did."

Dre pulled her hand from his to swipe a tear.

"I meant what I said before, Dre. Don't feel bad for me. And don't ever feel bad for choosing to leave. You did what you could for me, and did what you needed to do for you, and I admire you for it."

The swell of her throat threatened another sob, and the conflicts of her life now surfaced in her mind. Plans she'd had, now looking unclear. Feelings that had been unclear, now in crystalline focus. And a juxtaposition between the two.

"I'm a little jealous of you," she whispered.

"Jealous?"

"The clarity you have. I thought my life made sense. Now..."

Paul leaned back in his chair, a ghost of a grin on his face. "Now?"

His pause felt loaded. Like he knew but kind of enjoyed seeing her dangle in the space of discomfort. Brothers. Some things never changed.

While heat tipped her ears and washed over her face, she traced the grain on the wood table.

"This doesn't have anything to do Tom, does it?" The tease of his voice said he knew for certain it absolutely did.

"Shut up, Paul."

"What?" He laughed.

"Someday you'll know what it feels like, and then it won't

be so funny."

"Don't know about that. But pretty sure Tom likes you."

She snorted, and he laughed again. "That's good. Otherwise the phone calls, plane ticket, and kisses are really confusing."

"I don't need to know *all* of it."

Though her face grew warmer by the minute, she smirked. "What do you want to know?"

Paul crossed his arms and shrugged. "Nothing, I guess. Just, not really understanding the part about you being unclear. Seems like you've got a good thing with him, and I know you're doing awesome at school, so what's the problem?"

Dre sighed. "I liked my life in Texas. I saw my future there. Now..."

"You think Tom wouldn't leave Rock Creek?"

She shrugged. "I don't know. Not really something we've talked about—things aren't *that* serious." Except, she'd owned that she loved Tom. For her, they were that serious, and that felt as precarious as it did thrilling.

"Pretty sure for you, Dre, Tom would do about anything. Don't think you need to worry. If you want to stay in Texas, you two will figure it out."

"That's the thing."

"What?"

Dre pinned her lips. Why couldn't she say it out loud? It wasn't like she'd be betraying anyone. But if felt like...what? Failure? Like someone, somewhere, someday would point to her life and say, *You could have had the dream. You could have had it all. And instead...*

Paul stood, stepped around the table, and tugged Dre to her feet. "You know what, kid?" He pulled her into a strong hug while he spoke. "I know you're going to be fine. More than fine. You've always been faithful to listen to God, to seek His best in your life. Something that, even when I was being so stupid, I've really, really admired. You and Tom, you'll figure it out."

Tears. More stupid tears. Dre sniffed. "You think?"

"Don't doubt it for a minute. And I'll be praying for you."

Leaning back, Dre tipped her head so she could look at him. "That'd be good. Probably I should be doing more of that about it too."

"You haven't been?" Paul's eyebrows lifted.

He held her way too high in esteem, because on this, with her death grip on her life plans and her loosening grip on resentment of Tom's past, Dre hadn't been faithful to seek heaven's wisdom. Once again she was reminded how much she needed her Father in heaven. Such a contradiction, because she'd been acting like she was all good on her own.

With that in view, she took a fresh look at the fact that she was leaving in the morning. It'd be okay. Good. She and Tom would keep talking things through. Sharing their hearts and hopes and deepening what had been mostly chemistry up until Christmas.

And praying. Who knew God would use Paul to prod her toward that?

She squeezed him one last time. "I'm so glad you're here, Paul."

In so many ways, for so many reasons, she was glad.

Chapter Twenty-One

IT'D BEEN STUPID DARK WHEN THEY'D LEFT THAT MORNING.

Tom loaded Dre's single suitcase into the trunk of her mama's car—because once again Mama Rustin insisted he drive it rather than his pickup.

She'd slept over half the drive. Snuggled against his arm, warm and making him wish life would slow down for a minute so he could grab on to this amazing mystery forever. The past five days had spun in a whirlwind, and though none of it had been a vacation of any sort for Dre, he'd savored the time they'd shared. Quiet moments, her hand in his, while tears slipped over her nose. Long walks through the pastures out at the Rustin ranch, her at his side, asking him about what they did on the ranch, how he liked it, what he hoped to do with the Department of Natural Resources, and when he thought the position would open up.

And more tender moments. His heart rate picked up as his thoughts landed on those fresh memories, and he leaned to press a kiss against her thick mess of hair.

Man, he loved her. Wanted a hundred times at least to tell her. But she still hadn't touched the possibility of it, and the last thing he'd wanted for her was to feel pressure to say things she wasn't sure about.

So he'd take these moments. The ones where she looked at

him with depth, leaned on him like she appreciated his comfort, and confided in him like she'd someday give him her heart.

They'd stopped for a quick breakfast before he turned toward Denver International, and Dre told him about her visit with Paul the night before. Tears touched her voice when she said, "He's really okay, isn't he?"

"Yeah. Paul is doing well."

She leaned back against her seat, and with a glance, he saw her eyes squeeze shut.

"More than you hoped for?" he asked.

"Maybe not more than I'd hoped. At least, at some point. But maybe more than I honestly believed possible." She let a breathy, sad sort of laugh escape. "That's kind of faithless of me, isn't it?"

Tom didn't know what to say. Dre was the last person he'd label *faithless*.

"Do you know what's awesome?" she said.

"What's that?"

"God is so much bigger than I imagined. I kind of feel wonderstruck about it."

Tom laughed. "That is pretty awesome. Do you know what I think is awesome?"

He glanced her way, and she grinned.

"I can't believe the ways you find beauty and possibility in so many things in life. Most people don't, Dre. Not like you. And yet God still finds ways to hit you with wonder. That's pretty awesome." He took her hand, lifted her fingers to his mouth, brushed a kiss across her knuckles, and then held it.

God, I want to do life like this. Every day. Wonderstruck with her.

Once at the airport, he'd take her to passenger drop-off. Didn't like it, but she'd talked him into it. It was silly for him to pay for parking when she'd walk through the doors, check in, and have to say goodbye to him because he couldn't go past security with her. She was right, but he still hated it.

The winter sun seeped through the night, chasing shadows toward the mountains in the west when they turned into the airport maze and found their way to the correct drop-off point. Engine running, he popped the trunk while she gathered her backpack from the backseat. Nearby was a check-in counter, and he walked with her toward it, dragging her suitcase and holding her hand.

Too quickly, everything was in order. It was time for her to go. She'd walk through those doors, hop on a plane, and then...

What then?

He missed her already.

Stopping at a distance from the check-in counter but before the sliding doors, Tom tugged her hand, and she readily turned into him.

"Thank you, Tom," she breathed.

Her nose buried into his chest, stirring an ache that caught him off guard. Man, he loved this girl. Letting her go was painful.

Those words sat on his tongue, strong, demanding release. But she wasn't ready. Just, not yet. So he cradled her head, wrapped her close, held her tight. "I'll be missing you."

While her arms circled him, she tipped her face up to his. "Not for long, I hope."

What did that mean?

She pushed up to nip his mouth. "Spring break isn't far."

"Is that an invitation?" Better be an invitation. He was floating too high at the moment to handle that kind of emotional crash if it wasn't.

Shyness suddenly washed over her face as she rolled her lips together. "I'm sorry about Christmas," she whispered.

He smoothed her frown with the pad of his thumb, her lips soft beneath his touch. Too much to resist. The kiss was all him. And all her. All tender emotion. Enough to make him forget the passengers whisking by, sleepy but rushed to get through the security lines.

"Hey," came the bark of a man from somewhere behind. Tom lifted his face, instantly missing her mouth as the chill of January crashed against his. "This is a drop-off zone," a security officer said. "You're gonna have to say goodbye and move your car."

"Right. Sorry." Tom stepped back, his arms falling to his side, then lifted his hand to curve against Dre's face as he leaned for one last peck. "Bye, beautiful. I'll see you in a few weeks."

She smiled, relief softening her eyes.

Tom stepped away feeling his heart leave his chest as he moved. It was hers. All hers. It would be forever.

"Tom." Her voice caught him halfway back to the car. Strong. Maybe urgent.

He glanced at the security guy, who smirked and rolled his eyes but nodded, and Tom turned to Dre again.

The blue eyes he'd dreamed about nearly every night found his. Locked.

"I love you," she said. No shyness. No uncertainty.

It took a second. Or a minute. Maybe just a breath. Tom didn't know. But there she was, her bags left alone—another airport no-no—all tucked up against him, mouth deliciously moving with his.

And then she was sliding away again.

Not yet. With a gentle grab, he claimed her hand before she was gone.

He waited until her eyes met his again.

"I love you too."

She smiled. The best, most beautiful smile he'd ever seen, saved up for this exact moment.

He kissed her palm and let her go.

***

Dre landed on Texas soil with three certainties: God was at work, even if she hadn't been looking for it. She loved Tom and was certain she wanted her future tethered to his. And she really, really hated flying. The hot-footed, barely-made-it-without-totally-embarrassing-herself trip to the women's restroom after they landed put an exclamation mark on the last one.

For the love.

Janelle picked her up, stating in her charming southern drawl that Dre "looked about as fine as roadkill and might want to get better to die." Dre snickered, leaned into her friend's shoulder hug, and popped a mint Ice Cube from the box Tom had bought her.

The rest of the day she spent working on make-up assignments for the classes she'd missed, trying to push away the urge to call Tom every ten minutes. When he finally called her a little after nine, she sighed with relief.

He'd made it back to Rock Creek safely—his drive taking longer than her trip back to her dorm room, and how was that for fair? Not very, that was how. But he didn't complain. They talked about the upcoming week. About the winter storm moving toward Rock Creek. About the daffodils breaking ground outside her dorm, and how was that fair? It wasn't. Tom didn't complain.

"Hey, Dre?" Tom asked after forty-five minutes of nothing much but everything chatter.

"Yeah?"

"Did you mean it?"

She smiled and melted and wanted to be right there at his side. Even if a blizzard was heading that way. "Mean what?" she teased.

A groan tickled her ear, stirred her heart, and painted up

images of a warm fire, a snowstorm brewing outside, and Tom's arms cuddling her close, safe and sound. Why exactly had she come back to Texas?

"I meant it," she said, the heat of that imagined fire touching her skin. "I'm in love with you, Tommy Kent."

"You're sure?"

"As anything." More than anything, apparently, because the other things she'd been sure about had become uncertain in the light of this new thing with him.

His hesitation cooled the heat she'd just savored. "You okay?" she asked.

"Yeah, I'm good. And I love you too, Dre."

***

Tom couldn't bring himself to mention the email he'd found waiting in his inbox when he'd made it back to Rock Creek.

Tom, I wanted to give you a heads-up. I'm retiring, effective in May. You'll easily land the position, as you have my highest recommendation. The application process is simply a formality. The DNR Rock Creek branch will be proud to bring you on.

Glad I can leave knowing my work will continue with someone who loves this town, land, and its people as much as I do, and who walks and works with integrity. I'm looking forward to being able to announce your hire along with my retirement.

Sincerely, Jim Whitney

The job he'd been gunning for. All he could think about was telling Dre. She'd be proud of him—with the way she'd asked him about what that work would be and then talked about how he'd be so good at it, there was no doubt that she'd be proud. Excited for him. And then, well, she might draw some conclusions. Presumptions about what and where he thought their relationship should be. Wouldn't she?

They couldn't do this long-distance thing forever. He'd go

crazy. He'd barely survived putting her on a plane that morning and had already started counting the days until he'd get to see her again. Forty-three, in case she had a mind to check his honesty on that.

Thing was, Dre had plans of her own. Big plans that she'd be good at. Plans that wouldn't really thrive in the tiny speck of a town they'd grown up in the way they would where she'd planted new roots. How could he say he loved her the way he did and expect her to give that up?

He couldn't. So he didn't tell her. Instead, he started working at envisioning something different for himself. There was a lot of land in Texas. Surely he'd find something at a DNR branch down there. Or a ranch where he could be a hired hand. Or something.

Maybe he was getting way too far ahead of himself. Taking that *I love you* to mean bigger things than she'd meant at the moment. Just because he meant forever didn't mean she did.

In the middle of his mental twisting, which was a little bit of agony, by the way, Dre's comment from that morning came floating through his memory. *God is so much bigger than I imagined.*

Peace moved into the chaos. Once again, Dre found a way to point him toward beauty when he wasn't looking for it. So.

Tom turned the angst into prayer. Lifted up the crossroads where he'd found himself to the God who was indeed bigger than he'd imagined.

***

I have the lead on that project I was telling you about. It's fun. And stressful. Maybe I'm not built for business? I don't know. Mrs. Cooper says I'm doing well. Something in me though...
Miss you, Tom. And I love you.

***

Everybody has doubts when they're tired and stressed. You've had a bumpy start to this new year. Don't quit, Dre. I'm proud of you, and I know you've got this.
I love you too.

***

Tell me about home. About the ranch. How are your parents? My parents? Paul and Grams? I miss everyone so much. Mostly you.
I counted the days. Thirty-two. You're coming still, right? Please come.

***

Yes, I'm coming. Everyone is well, for the most part. Paul is neck deep in calving season. Your Grams looks smaller every day. I think her heart is already gone. I stay out at the ranch a couple nights a week to give Paul a break from calving. Guess what? That "bunkhouse" is freezing. Paul said that would make you laugh. Hope so. I want you to smile.

***

You stayed in the bunkhouse? Yikes.
Paul said that he felt like Grams would follow Pop soon. It's bittersweet. And thinking about her and Pop makes me look at my life with a different lens.
Tom, something is off in me. Everything is going awesome. I'm nailing this project. Mrs. Cooper asked to meet me for lunch at the end of the week, and she was smiling when she did, so that's a good thing. I think. But all I can think about is going home. I've been here four years, and that's never happened. I want to blame you. What have you done to me? *insert wink and smile* But it isn't just you. I dream about the ranch. About the barn in town. About working in the kitchen with Mama.
What is wrong with me? I've worked like crazy for the opportunities that are opening up in front of me. Part of me is

*taking a big old pause. Wondering why success is so important.
I've never stopped to think about it. It was always drive harder,
work more. Now I'm stepping back, asking questions. It's like
there are empty places in me that push me to perfection. Success.*

Are you freaking out? I might be. A little

Don't freak out. I need you to not freak out.

***

*Not freaking out. Missing you, wishing I could hold your
hand through this conversation. But not because I'm freaking
out.*

*I think we all have those empty places that drive us. Part of
the reason I did the dumb stuff I did in high school.*

*What if those empty places are really gifts, Dre? What if
they're like windows that, if we stopped trying to fill them—
plug them up or cover them over—they would be the places that
would let the Son shine in?*

*I meant what I told you before. I'm proud of you and your
hard work. But you don't need to be successful for me to be
proud of you. I love your heart, Dre. It's what I want most.*

***

With the calming backdrop of the river playfully tumbling
over rocks, the mid-seventies warmth of early spring on her
face, and the smell of the earth coming alive after a short
winter's nap, Dre settled against the slab of Texas stone that
made a natural bench. She had a little more than an hour
before she would meet Mrs. Cooper for lunch. A little more
than an hour to get a handle on what she wanted.

Who was she kidding? For years she had a clear picture. Now,
for the past two months, her vision had come unraveled. How
unfair was that? Falling in love shouldn't be this complicated,
should it? And yet, Tom reentered her life, and though she was
incredibly happy with him, everything else shifted.

Drawing a deep breath, Dre lifted her phone and opened the

string of emails she and Tom had exchanged and read them through yet again.

What if those empty places were really gifts?

Was that even possible? If she stopped trying to fill the holes that had suddenly surfaced within her, would the light pour in instead? Would she find the peace that had suddenly fled?

Are these empty parts from You?

What was God saying to her in them? Why couldn't she understand?

Answers didn't come pouring in. Instead, there was the gentle tumbling of the river. The rich smell of spring coming to life. And the sun on her face. There she sat in a picturesque scene, but when she shut her eyes, her heart went elsewhere.

She saw a white-clad farmhouse. A small pond in the distance, and beyond that, a stretch of pasture that met a rich green hayfield. She knew this spot, and it wasn't in Texas.

When her time ran short and she needed to go meet her professor, Dre was still left with questions. And longings. But now those longings had a name—and it wasn't what she'd expected.

Home. She ached to go home.

Chapter Twenty-Two

THE BAKERY MRS. COOPER HAD SUGGESTED WAS ADORABLE.

It would be. Mrs. Cooper had overseen the remodel. White tile. Butcher-block tables with metal farm chairs surrounding them. A clean glass case displaying the delicious offerings of this local treasure. Framed prints of nature, and black vinyl letters scrawled over a clean white wall, spelling out *bless this gathering*.

Dre brushed the remains of her crescent roll from her fingers and sat back, finding Mrs. Cooper's smile ready.

"Remember before Thanksgiving, when I told you that I try to listen to Jesus?" she asked, folding her hands on the table and leaning forward.

Not sure where this little turn was going, Dre forced her shoulders to relax. "Yeah…"

"You've been on my mind quite a bit, Andrea. Partly because I'm very pleased with both your work and your ability to engage with people. We've already talked about how important that is. To be honest, I would love to offer you a position with me when you graduate."

A thrill pulsed through Dre—an electric current of success and pride. But at the tail of it, there was also a sense of hesitancy. The same one that had been pestering her for weeks.

Dre scooted closer to the table. "I'm so excited about that," she started. She should follow that up with something about how she'll work hard. Keep pursuing excellence...

"I sense a *but*." Mrs. Cooper lifted her brows, waited a moment, and then smiled gently. "And that's why I opened this conversation the way I did. Andrea, the selfish part of me wants to snatch you up, even if that means pressuring you with a seize-the-moment speech. But the thing is, life is complex. I sense a shift in you that shouldn't be ignored."

Panic rose. Had her work slipped? Had she become melancholy, and that made Mrs. Cooper second-guess her sort-of extended offer? "If I've disappointed you, I'm—"

"Not at all. If anything, you keep getting better. I'm not sure there are words to tell you what I mean. I've had a whisper in my heart, a nudging to share some things that I've found along the way. Maybe they'll be useful to you. Maybe not."

"About design?" Dre asked.

"No. About life. A perspective you likely won't hear from many other women. One you might strongly disagree with, and that's okay. But I hope you won't be offended by what I say. As I began, I've felt a nudge to share with you, and if what I say at all gives you the freedom to make whatever decision I think you might be struggling with, then it's worth the risk to share."

"Okay..."

Mrs. Cooper could see that Dre was struggling? She couldn't even pinpoint the choice she needed to make, exactly. How did the other woman know it was there?

"Here's the thing." Mrs. Cooper settled back in her chair. "Sometimes our culture tells us as women that we can have it all. The implication is that we can have it all *at once*. My life has taught me that is a lie, and it's a stressful one when you're trying to make it happen. Dre, there are only so many hours in a day, and we can only do so much. What's one of the first things you learn about in economics and investing?"

Classes Dre had taken for her business minor, so the answer came fairly easy. "There are always opportunity costs. Wise investors have to look at them and weigh the potential gain against the loss."

"Exactly. That's true of life." Mrs. Cooper sighed. "A fact I didn't realize until stress and frustration and the constant feeling of failure had squeezed the joy out of my dreams and almost took the life out of my marriage. See, when I was in my twenties, newly married and my head full of dreams, I was completely absorbed in the idea that I could do it all. Have it all. If I worked hard enough. Did more. Did whatever it took. It was exhausting. Long story short, I came to a place where I realized that I had to let something go. It was kind of devastating, and I felt like I was such a failure. Why couldn't I do it all when Oprah said I could and so many other women apparently were?

"Bottom line? It didn't matter. I needed to make some choices, because something was going to give. My health. My marriage. My family. Or my job. Or they were all going to crash. Those choices, they were hard. I won't lie. Letting go of the dreams I'd chased felt a little bit like a death to me. But then, after the grieving began to ease, I was able to see past the moment. I was healthy again. My family wasn't in constant chaos. And I began to see new opportunities open up."

Dre filtered through Mrs. Cooper's story, trying to piece what she knew of the woman now with what she was saying. It didn't add up. "But you run one of the most successful design firms in the state," she blurted.

Mrs. Cooper nodded, her smile gentle. "I do now. But do you know how old my company is?"

Dre stopped short. No, actually. She didn't.

"Live Oak Design is only ten years old, Dre. The dream of it? That's been over twenty-five years in the making."

Oh.

The pieces fell into place. Oh.

"But...putting things off? I mean, what if this opportunity never comes again?"

"Who's to say? What you do know now, what I suspect has shifted in you, is that there's a cost. Something you've found that maybe is worth more than the dream you thought was so important. We may not be able to have it all, but we can sure love what we have. Or maybe, better put, who we have." She winked, a knowing smile curving her mouth.

Dre's eyes shifted from the table to Mrs. Cooper, only just now aware that she'd spoken her thoughts out loud.

With a warm, kind hand, Mrs. Cooper gripped hers. "I'm in no position to tell you or any other young, ambitious woman what to do. You have the talent to do many things. I've found that even when talent is abundant, time is scarce. Doing things well required me to make choices. I made mine, and though they were hard at the time, I don't regret them for one moment now. But my story isn't yours, and you get to choose for yourself. I wanted to share with you a perspective that maybe you don't hear in this loud world of do-it-all women. Know that my offer is sincere. If you want a place with Live Oak, I'd love to have you. But my heart is also sincere, and should you choose something else, I wholeheartedly respect that too."

***

Paul's phone call the day before Tom's arrival didn't initially seem strange. Her brother had called her every now and then since Thanksgiving. He was determined to rebuild the relationship they'd lost, and Dre loved him for it.

But as they moved past the normal *how are things and people and stuff*, Paul paused, and Dre sensed a hesitation.

"What's going on, Paul?"

"Uh..."

She could imagine him running a hand over his hair, if he was inside without his hat on.

"I felt like maybe there was something you needed to know. Maybe you already do."

Her stomach twisted. This was about Tom. She knew it. And though she already knew about Tom's past, she didn't love the idea of discussing it with Paul. Truthfully, there were still stains of resentment and hurt she was working through, and the added stab of shame that she should struggle so much with it. *Love keeps no record of wrongs...* She'd cling to that and had begun praying for God to give her a heart of real love. The kind that lived in humility and extended forgiveness. The kind that had to soak in heaven's love first.

"Look." Paul's voice filled the silent void Dre had allowed. "I know you and Tom are grown-up people and can handle your own stuff, but I have a feeling he hasn't told you."

"Paul."

"No, Dre, you should know, and I need to make sure of it. He's sure he's doing the right thing, but won't tell me for certain he's talked to you about it."

"Paul, you're right. We're grown up and can deal with our own stuff."

"So you know he's not even going to apply for Jim Whitney's position?"

"Wait. What?"

"Jim is retiring, effective the end of May. Tom's wanted that job since he graduated high school. I get it if you two have things worked out, and you're going to stay in Texas, and he doesn't want to keep this long-distance thing up. But, Dre—"

"He's not even applying?"

Paul paused. "No. So you didn't know."

"He..." Her heart plummeted. Tom hadn't said a word. Not one thing about it in any of their emails or phone calls. Why wouldn't he tell her?

"Dre." Paul inhaled, the draw of breath loud enough to carry over the phone. "He really loves you. I think probably you love him. I'm not telling you two what to do, but I didn't think it was right for him to decide things without you."

"Maybe he was going to tell me this week." She latched on to that with all the strength of a feather. But defense rang in her voice.

"Okay. I'm out of it." Paul apparently heard her irritation.

A sigh sagged through her, heavy enough to sink her farther into the cushions of her couch. "Don't be like that, Paul. Thanks for telling me. I'm just not sure what to think."

"I'm sure he didn't do it to hurt you, Dre."

"I know." Certainly Tom had done it to protect her. To show her that he'd chase her dreams right by her side. Problem was, those dreams that had been everything before had morphed. Slipped into something new and simpler, and she hadn't yet reconciled the shift enough to make sense.

They had some things to talk about.

***

The sunshine was friendly and made the trail off the parking lot seem a little bit like a gateway to paradise. Tom reached for Dre's hand as he came around the nose of his pickup, and when she sidled beside him, her fingers lacing with his, this paradise felt complete for the moment.

"So this is the favorite spot?" They passed under a giant live oak, its sprawling branches an arbor that somehow felt like magic.

"Yes." Dre sighed as though peace had overtaken the strain he'd sensed in her since he'd arrived that morning.

Hand in hand, they strolled down the trail. The path dropped a little, then curved when it met the edge of the river.

Dots of yellow and white—daffodils and snowdrops—jumped to life against the dark soil and stone that the river's extended boundary had exposed. The smell of damp earth, the sounds of moving water, and a breeze rustling through the light-green buds ready to burst at the tips of the trees, all added to the enchantment.

"I can see why." Tom had been hard pressed to imagine a place Dre loved more than the river property. Hadn't banked on this. But here they were, and the love she clearly had for this spot was like a silent confirmation. He'd made the right decision.

She led him to a place where the stacked stone made a natural bench overlooking a bend in the water's trail. Sliding onto the seat beside her, he released the hand he held and curled his arm around her. She was his. She loved him, and he loved her, and he could learn to love this place like she did. For her. It shouldn't be too hard.

In the stillness between them, Dre leaned in against him. As he pressed a kiss against the top of her head, the words *perfect moment* scrawled through his mind. He could tell her. Then the stab of guilt that had been jabbing him about keeping something from her would go away. They could move forward, maybe make some plans together.

Yes. This perfect moment was a good one to start with. But when he nudged her, cupping her face with his hand to bring her eyes to his, the words to begin that conversation evaporated. The draw to her mouth pulled him. Kissing was so much easier.

She seemed to agree.

After who knew how long but definitely not long enough, she paused. Breathless, she pulled away, and a groan of protest escaped his lips.

"I'm gonna marry you, Dre." Head still pressed to hers, the words whisked from his chest on a ragged breath.

She chuckled. "That so?"

"Oh, I wanna." He moved to focus his gaze on her.

Face beautifully flushed, a smile that yanked his heart clean through his chest and landed it in her palms spread across the lips he'd just thoroughly explored.

"Maybe. If you ask nice."

He caught that soft mouth again. Then kissed her nose. Her cheek. Her forehead. "Plan on it."

Once again she leaned away, though her hands still gripped the button-down that would certainly tattle on them to the world with its no-longer-pressed condition. The gleam of passion and joy faded from those baby-blue eyes, and the mouth that had been smiling drew downward.

"What?" he asked.

"You're not going to tell me, are you?"

Oh no. The perfect moment had slipped by. Because kissing was way more fun. "Tell you..." Playing dumb. Good idea. Should work out well.

Her hands fell to her lap, jaw stiffened, and she turned to face the river. "Really, Tom? You weren't even going to talk about it with me?"

Silence seemed like the best option. How did she know about the job? Maybe this was about something else, and he really was innocent.

Because that made sense.

"Mr. Whitney is retiring." She shot a glare at him. "The job you've been wanting forever. And you didn't even apply."

Caught. Was not saying anything the same thing as lying?

Paul and his big fat mouth. Tom had told him to stay out of it. Told him they were grown-ups and could manage their own lives. Paul had shaken his head, shot him a *you're looking for trouble* kind of glare, and gone on in silent reproof, spreading cane from the bale they'd delivered to the new cattle pairs.

"Look, Dre." Tom scrambled for the right thing to say

while dousing irritation with her brother. Trying to douse. Wasn't working, by the frustration in his voice. He gripped her shoulders.

She spun against the stone to meet him with an intense glare. "Don't *look Dre* me, Tommy Kent. I'm a big girl, and I know when I'm being treated otherwise. You want to marry me? Not like this. You don't get to decide my future for me."

What on earth? "Dre, I did it for you. Because I'd like to live in the same zip code the woman I plan to marry claims as her home. How can you be angry about that?"

"You didn't talk to me!" Tears sheened her eyes, but didn't make her look any less angry. "Why would you assume I'd expect you to give up everything you've worked toward for me? Do you think I'm that spoiled? Self-centered?"

"No." His heart rate spiked. "No, I don't think that about you. And I sure didn't want you to think that about me. I know what you've got going here. I know that you feel like this is home now. What kind of a man would I be if I made you give that up?"

Why was this a fight? The fact that he kept if from her aside, she shouldn't be angry about it. Should she? And yet.

She shot to her feet. Paced away. Crossed her arms. Gave him her back.

Whether she should be or not, she was hoppin' mad.

He crammed a hand into his thick hair and studied her straight back. Looked a whole lot like it did that night beside Harper's Pond—about as soft as a fence post. The other time she'd gotten super angry after he'd kissed her. That, he understood. This? He had a sinking sensation that he'd never really figure her out. Which was frustrating.

Oh, but he loved her. The thought eased his exasperation. A little.

"Dre, I wanted to show you that I'm serious. Maybe it's too soon and you're not ready. Maybe that's what's really freaking you out about this."

She spun, eyes wide, jaw set. "What?" Her march toward him stamped very clearly that he'd absolutely said the wrong thing. "I'm freaked out because you made a huge decision about something that would impact our future—together—without talking to me. You weren't even going to bring it up."

"Yes I was."

"When?"

Would *now* be a valid answer? *I got distracted kissing you.* Yeah, that'd go over really well. Pulse strumming heat through him, Tom studied her. Fought his own anger while watching hers blaze.

This whole thing was ripe for an explosion. Tom wasn't the fighting kind. That had been Paul's thing. Tom? He preferred peace, and evasion figured into that. Thus, the not telling her about the job thing.

Maybe she had a little room to be angry. He had felt guilty about keeping it from her, so there was something in him that knew she should be a part of that decision. But in his defense, he thought the fight would be the other way. That she'd work to convince him to *not* apply. That she wanted life here in Texas, and the strain between their two divergent life plans would be uncomfortable at best. He'd thought he'd avoided the whole issue, and wasn't that chivalrous of him?

So back to being mad right back at her.

Still didn't want this argument to blow up though. Tom rubbed his neck, looked to the ground while he inhaled. Twice. He could be the peacemaker. An apology, and they'd move on...

"I'm sorry, Dre. I thought I was making the right choice. I thought we'd avoid an argument, and you'd know that I want you to find the success you've been hunting for."

She softened. A little. Her arms fell to her sides, and she bit her bottom lip, which quivered a tiny bit. "Tom, it's your life too. And I'm not fragile."

"I know you're not."

"Then why are you afraid of this?"

"Of what?"

"I can see you're still angry. I can hold my own in a discussion. I'm not a wimp, so don't cover over what you're thinking because you'd rather have peace than deal with the problem."

Holy smokes, was she serious? "You're determined to have a fight, aren't you?"

"If it means we're honest with each other, then yeah."

He shook his head. "You're making me nuts right now, Dre."

"Then it's mutual."

Words would not form. Tom stared at her, dumbfounded. She held his gaze, silently challenging him.

Well then.

"Okay. Be honest," he said. "Tell me why there's steam rolling from your ears about this. I made a choice I thought would be best for us. For you. I had no idea you'd be livid about it."

"Exactly. You decided. All by yourself. Didn't talk to me about it, and weren't going to tell me. Meanwhile, apparently everyone in Rock Creek knows, including my brother. You just assumed you knew what I'd think. Assumed you knew what I'd want."

"Fine." He stepped closer. "What do you want, Andrea Rustin?"

That touched something. Anger shifted to confusion in her expression as tears slipped over her eyes. The place of hardness that had been gripping his chest shattered, leaving him with only an ache. Lifting both hands, he framed her face, caught the rolling tears with his thumb. "Dre?"

She broke. Cried for real. It didn't make sense, but it still broke his heart. "Dre, what do you want?"

"I don't know," she whispered.

Alarms rolled through his mind. This. This was what he'd been trying to avoid. But maybe she was right—maybe they shouldn't avoid the hard conversations.

He swallowed. Drew a deep breath. "You don't know...about us?"

She bolted into his chest, the arms circling him fierce. "No. I know I want this. Us. It's everything else I don't know about. I thought I saw everything so clearly. But now I'm homesick all the time, and the sense of satisfaction I had in my work is draining away. I can't see me here anymore, but I'm having a hard time letting go of that vision." Her forehead pressed against him, and then she tipped her wet face up to look at him. "That doesn't make sense, does it?"

Tom drew her closer, strengthened his hold. *Note to self: When this woman got this mad, there might be more than one storm brewing. Be quick to listen, slow to speak, and slow to become angry. And don't assume he knew what she wanted.*

Some big revelations there. Probably stuff he'd have to relearn all over again, many times over, because this relationship thing was like learning how to waltz—which he didn't actually know how to do. The steps looked complicated, counting seemed confusing, and the music, while pretty, messed the whole thing up more.

But this waltz with Dre—the one of life? That he was willing to learn. Stumble through only to reset and try again.

For now, she'd cry. He'd hold her. And then they could figure the problem out. Together.

Chapter Twenty-Three

THEY HADN'T REALLY FIGURED ANYTHING OUT, BUT DRE
FELT A LITTLE BETTER WHEN TOM DROPPED HER OFF AT THE
DORM LATER THAT AFTERNOON.

She had some homework she needed to get done and a four-
hour shift at the diner. Tom had been easy about that. Said
he'd check into his hotel, get a shower and a much-needed nap
after that thirteen-hour drive. They'd go out for a late dinner.
And talk.

They needed to talk more.

She paused at the mirror where she'd stopped to pin her
blond hair up in a work-ready messy bun and shut her eyes.
What do I want? Her thoughts shifted upward. *What do You
want?*

It'd be so much easier if God would give her a vision. And
Tom the same vision. Then they'd be on the same page and
wouldn't have to wade through hard choices that made for
strained conversations and frustrating moments.

But then, that was life, wasn't it? If they wanted one
together—and they did—they'd have to figure this out. One
hard choice at a time. One awkward conversation at a time.

She plowed into her homework, got it done, and walked her
way down to the diner where she waitressed. Time moved
slowly. When Tom finally came through the jingling door to

pick her up, she thought she'd fly into his arms and soak in a kiss that she hadn't been able to enjoy in almost six whole hours.

For the love. She was ridiculous.

Instead, she put on her grown-up face, met his smile with her own, and tried to pretend the look he gave her didn't about make her knees buckle. After she clocked out, said good night to the shift manager, and slipped her arms through her white sweater, she slipped her hand into Tom's, and he walked her to his pickup.

She about thought he didn't miss her as much as she did him until he stopped her from climbing into the cab and claimed her mouth as soon as she turned to see what was the matter. There was no pretending about the knee thing then.

"So you did miss me," she whispered when a sliver of night air spread between them.

"You doubted?"

"Well..."

"You're almost all I think about. Kind of why you need to marry me."

"You keep saying that word..."

Tom chuckled, and then his stomach rumbled. Dre stepped from his arms as she laughed.

"Almost all." She winked.

His grin was little boy—and slightly self-conscious, because this man she loved was the shy sort. Even when he flirted. Heaven must have blessed that, because it sure melted her heart.

She pushed him away and hopped into the cab. "Let's go eat."

Tom asked where to go, and she directed him to a small barbeque joint. By the time their food was ordered and drinks served, her stomach was rumbling too.

"You could have picked something nicer." Tom stretched his

arm across the booth table and snatched her hand.

"As in *fancy?*"

He shrugged.

"Do you know who you're dealing with here? I grew up in Nebraska."

"Doesn't mean you can't go somewhere a little more upscale than barbeque."

Appreciation swelled in her, because he meant it as a compliment. "This suits me, cowboy."

The conversation during dinner was easy. Like the phone calls they made every night. Except Dre could watch the way Tom's eyes would darken or widen or dance with whatever was being said at the moment. And feel his knees brush hers. But they didn't return to the topic that had turned heated until near the end of the meal.

It had to be said though.

"Tom, I think you should apply." Dre knew it was an abrupt turn from the story she'd told him about dropping an entire tray of drink orders for a table of eight her first week waitressing. But she also knew he'd follow. "I want you to."

Tom wiped his mouth with a well-smeared napkin, taking his time, clearly thinking about his words before he aired them. Slowly he slid his hand across the table and brushed her knuckles with the tips of his fingers. "What if I can't take the job, Dre?"

She heard the subtext. The questions he didn't ask. What if you change your mind? What if you want to stay here?

That would imply that she'd made up her mind. She hadn't. Mostly hadn't. Now that the topic was out in the open again, time seemed to press against her. Maybe against them both. He needed to be fair to the people at the Rock Creek Department of Natural Resources. Which meant that she needed to figure out what she wanted.

Or they needed to take a step backward.

No pressure.

"I can see you panicking." He lifted her fingers. "This isn't supposed to be pressure. That's why I didn't tell you—not that I'm trying to excuse it."

"But I don't want you to miss this opportunity. It's what you wanted."

He shrugged. "Sometimes what we thought we were after shifts."

"Yeah." Boy, did she know that.

The heaviness of the topic settled between them, and Dre absently ran her thumb along his index finger. Honesty began to lift in her—the budding truth that she wasn't sure was truly honest. But there it was, nudging her tongue until she set the words free.

"What if I want to go home?"

Again he shrugged, as if that possibility wasn't monumental. "Then we'll go home." He lifted her hand, brushed her knuckles against his lips. "Is that what you want, Dre?"

"I told you, I don't know."

"Anyone for dessert tonight?"

Their waiter snatched the intensity from the moment, startling Dre.

Oblivious, he smiled. "The molten lava is not to be missed, in case you're wondering."

"Want to share?" Tom lifted an eyebrow.

Because, actually, yes she did. And clearly he did, in fact, know who he was dealing with here.

Tom grinned. "Bring us one."

"Two spoons?" the guy in all black asked.

Duh. Otherwise the cowboy across the table might eat more than his fair share.

Left alone again, Tom leaned back against the padded seat. "How about we table this? No big decisions tonight, okay?"

"Table it until when?"

"Until it seems like there might be a solution."

"What if that's never?"

"It won't be never."

"What if it's too late?"

"For what?"

"For you to apply for that job you've been wanting for like five years."

Tom sighed, his left hand gripping his neck.

"I really want you to apply, Tom."

"And I really want you to finish this term project you're doing so well at before you make any decisions you might come to regret."

Dre tensed. "I'm not going to regret being with you."

"That's not what I meant." He shifted, his arms spreading out on the table, taking up most of the space as he leaned in. "Home for me can be here. It can be wherever you are. I promise, Dre. I'll be content. There'll be other jobs. Other opportunities."

How could she not love this man?

The guy with their molten lava arrived. Perfect timing, again. The rich dark chocolate oozed against the white of the vanilla ice cream, and the garnish of strawberries made the entire deal irresistible. Even during an impasse.

Chocolate didn't solve anything.

They tabled it. But at least they'd talked. And when Tom kissed her good night at the door to her dorm, all traces of tension melted between them. Kind of like that vanilla ice cream.

"I love you," he whispered as his mouth feathered her cheek.

For that night, it was enough.

***

For all the exhaustion he felt from the trip, Tom couldn't

fall asleep.

He'd put her off again. For the best though, right? This was the right decision. How could he apply for a job he may not be able to take? Or may want to quit right after getting started?

Slow down.

Those two words had been skulking through his mind uninvited all afternoon. As much as he'd tried to corner them, expel them, or simply ignore them, there they were. Seeping into his thoughts like a stubborn theme song looping through his mind.

Fine. Slow what down, exactly?

Things had gone fast with Dre. Was that a problem? He'd known he was in love with her. And he had no reason to question whether she was truthful with her claim. Dre wouldn't say something like that if she didn't mean it clear through. She wasn't the type to mess around with her life or anyone else's.

He was going to marry her. *Right? I mean, that's okay, right?*

Funny. He'd prayed over everything else concerning her. From *Please bring her back. Just once.* To, *Help me to let her go.* To, *Show me how to tell her how I feel.* Every piece had been ironed out and made smooth.

Hadn't thought to pray about this though. The riot in his mind settled, and he shut his eyes against the dark loneliness of the hotel room. There was a King of all things in heaven and earth Who knew the beginning from the end, the number of hairs on his head, and how few he'd likely have when it came to the last days of his life. These questions he and Dre had were best brought before the One who had known them and loved them before either had drawn their first breath.

So Tom started there. With the question most pressing in his heart.

Can I marry her?

Chapter Twenty-Four

She was allowed to cry, right?

For all those people who said a girl in love was sappy and weepy, well. Just well. They weren't her, and the love of her life done just drove north without her. So she could cry about it if she wanted to.

Maybe that was a little dramatic. He did tell her he loved her before he left. Kissed her soundly, something of which he'd done quite a bit during his four-day visit. And left her with the sweetest almost-a-proposal ever.

Dre let that moment roll through her mind as she leaned against the dorm room door. He'd knelt right there by that shelf rock bench near the river where they'd gone every day during his visit. Lifted her hand. Looked into her eyes with those steel blues she kind of loved a lot.

Her heart had skipped and hopped and sang and danced right along with the playful river and happy birds. The perfect moment.

"Will you..."

Dramatic pause. Was this Tom? Her Tom? Tommy Kent, Paul's shy, sort-of sometimes ornery friend who'd kissed her? Quite a lot these days?

He grinned. The ornery-boy sort. Not the shy sort. "Promise to go ring shopping with me someday down the road so I can propose to you properly when the time is right?"

For. The. Love.

She'd shoved him to his backside. Laughing. Tom had laughed too.

Even now, alone in her dorm room, little tears of sappy sadness tracing her cheeks because Tom had left, the scene made her laugh.

"So."

Dre jolted off the door, barely bottling a yelp.

Janelle snickered. "You kind of like this Tom guy, huh?"

"What are you doing here?" Dre grabbed at her shirt, hoping her heart had stayed inside her chest.

"I live here, remember?" Janelle's grin spread. Her amused eyes danced. "And also, remember how you weren't supposed to fall for that guy? You made me promise not to let you fall for that guy."

Dre faked a swoon. "I can't help myself."

Laughing, Janelle pushed her over to the couch, where Dre flopped, hand over her head. "He's not so bad then?"

Shutting her eyes, Dre smiled. "He's going to marry me."

"Whoa." Janelle pushed Dre's legs out of the way so she could sit. "He proposed? Where the ring?"

"No ring. And not a real proposal. Yet."

Janelle's forehead wrinkled, but after a moment of weird staring, she shook her head. "You are some strange northern ducks. But I'm happy for you. And also, I told you so."

Dre shifted so she could lean against her friend's shoulder.

"What about Live Oak?" Janelle asked, her tone gentle.

"Tami Cooper offered me a job after graduation. If I want it."

"Did you tell Tom?"

"Yeah."

"Thought you were all mad earlier this week because your brother told you he turned down the job he wanted up there."

"Yeah. I was."

"You're not making any sense."

Dre pushed upright and turned to face Janelle. "What if I didn't take the job with Live Oak? Would you say I was crazy? Wasting my life? Throwing away the biggest opportunity?"

"That's a lot of things to say." Janelle perched her elbow on the back side of the couch. The laughter in her dark eyes simmered as she studied Dre. "I'd say sometimes a pup just knows when she needs to go home."

Dre rolled her eyes. "You say the weirdest things ever."

"You love me for it."

Latching on to Janelle's arm, Dre snuggled with her. "You know I do. But I'm still not sure what I'm doing."

"Did Tom ask you to come home?"

"No. He told me to focus on this project. To make it amazing, like he knows I can. And then we'll see."

"Sounds like a good plan."

"*We'll see* isn't much of a plan."

"Hmm."

Dre waited for more. Expected another strange packed-full-of-wisdom saying that only Janelle could spout off the cuff. But it didn't come.

For now then, she'd focus on making this design project the best she could. And then maybe they'd find answers when they got there.

***

Waiting for clarity still wasn't Tom's favorite game. It was too much like patience, and he hadn't nailed that one yet. But he got one thing for sure—Dre was upset that he hadn't applied, and that mattered.

After praying about it, and hearing Dre say at least three times over the past four days that she really thought he should apply, Tom decided he needed to have a conversation with Jim Whitney. He'd lay out the problem. Ask the older man for his opinion, and go from there.

Jim listened, his face neutral. And then after Tom's explanation, he nodded. "I wondered what was going on. Had heard all kinds of rumors that you were joining the army. Or moving to Canada. Running from a broken heart or something."

"Who said that?"

Jim laughed. "You know small towns. Everyone thinks they know something about somebody."

"Huh."

"So you still want the job, but you're not sure how long or even if you can accept it, because Andrea Rustin has a pretty good opportunity elsewhere, and you think you might not be able to live without her?"

Sounded cheesy stated like that. Tom cleared his throat, gripped the back of his neck.

Again, Jim chuckled. "Loving a woman is nothing to be ashamed of, Tom. I get it. But she still thinks you should apply?"

"Yeah."

"Sounds like she might love you back."

That didn't require an answer.

"I think she's right," Jim continued. "Apply. And if the job is offered, which is highly likely, take it. There are opportunities to transfer. It may not be on your ideal timeline, but you'd be within the system, which would be good."

Transfer? Hadn't thought of that. Still. Tom rubbed his jawline. "I hate the thought of leaving the people here in a bad spot."

"Give enough notice if things shift toward Texas. I know you won't up and leave without fair warning." Jim stood and gripped Tom's shoulder. "It'll work out, Tom. Sometimes you've got to give a snag a little bit of slack. It'll sort itself."

Another way of saying those two words that had pressed in his mind in Texas. *Slow down.* Or, be patient. Wait and see.

Not things he was good at.

***

Spring moved like the thawing waters on a mountain. Slow at first, and then as April brought longer days with warmer sunshine, the meltdown became swift waters.

Not that Dre's current address had mountains. Or her previous one, for that matter. Just something she'd learned when she spent a summer working at a camp in Colorado. And thought about as her life became more like those rushing rivers.

She put herself into full-on design mode as her project neared the May 1 deadline. Her other classes received enough attention that she would maintain her high marks through graduation, but the bulk of her energy went into nailing the design Mrs. Cooper had put her in charge of. And her efforts were paying off.

This project wasn't hypothetical. It was hands on, the real deal, and in a week, the owner would walk through the house she'd poured her best creative energies into. Every room would have her ideas brought to full life. Her touch.

Which meant every room was open to criticism.

As much as she pushed that possibility to the back of her mind, she couldn't completely remove it. Cold sores formed in her mouth—symptoms of the stress she had flooding her body. When she slept, she saw the project. When she ate, she thought about what needed tweaking. Or about what might go wrong. The snags they'd encountered along the way—which Mrs. Cooper had warned would be inevitable and was part of the job—had robbed some sleep.

Still, she loved what she was doing. The anticipation of seeing her vision brought forth in real life was thrilling.

Along the way, she'd shared her fears, thrills, frustrations, and triumphs with Tom. He never wavered in his support. Even on the Tuesday in mid-April when he told her he'd been offered the job with the DNR.

Dre had squealed. Clapped her hands as she said, "I knew it!"

Tom laughed, said he'd asked for two weeks to really consider if he could accept. An odd move in most situations, but since Tom had explained things to Mr. Whitney, and the older man's retirement wasn't until the end of May, the office had agreed.

"Focus on crushing this design, okay, Dre?" he'd said. "This job situation will work out."

It was humbling to be loved like that. Dre dwelled on that the night before the house reveal, when she couldn't sleep. Tom had put things on hold—she suspected even a real proposal—so that she wouldn't feel the pressure of this decision she needed to make. At least, not from him. She thought about the quiet way he loved her, and those thoughts wound back to the still-present prick of hurt she felt when she remembered what had happened five years ago.

Love keeps no record of wrong.

Learning to let go of those things was hard, and that still frustrated her. But Janelle had been right—God hadn't shunned her efforts, small and stumbling as they were. The big hurts and the little hurts, they mattered to her God. He invited her to bring them to Him. Wanted her to. It was really like what Tom had said—those holes were more like windows if she'd stop covering them over and let the Son shine in.

The day of the reveal started with those thoughts, which turned to a sweet prayer. *Please, let Your light shine in me.*

Whatever else in her life, Dre gripped that. It was the strongest want in her. What if Jesus could be her everything? That kind of life would be successful, no matter where she was or what she was doing.

That right there was her calling.

Calm took the place of anxiety. Which wasn't to say that she wasn't nervous. Maybe a strange contradiction, but true nonetheless. She'd present her work, the best efforts she could give on that project. Hopefully, their client would love it. Either way, though, she had her answer.

She knew what was next.

**

"You really hit this one out of the park." Beaming, Tami Cooper hugged Dre. "Not that I had any doubt along the way. But wow. This was fantastic."

Dre swallowed, blinking back the joy that threatened to brim over her eyelids. It'd been a rush, watching her client take in the work they'd done, the space they'd created, and loving every bit of it. "Thank you, Mrs. Cooper, for trusting me with this. It was an amazing experience."

Tami Cooper stepped back, pride still shining in her eyes. "Have you made a decision about my offer?"

A tiny pang thrust in Dre's chest. Not of doubt or even of regret for what she was about to say. But of simply the reality that this chapter was going to close. By her choice, and she was sure of it, but ends were always hard.

"I have." She pulled in a deep breath. "It's time for me to go home. I'm so grateful for every opportunity you've given me, Mrs. Cooper, and what an honor it would be to work for Live Oak, but I've decided to go home."

"You're sure?"

Dre met her eyes and nodded.

Tami gripped her hand, her smile more emotional than Dre had ever seen. "I'm sure you'll have the adventure of a lifetime, wherever you go. Whatever you do. And if there's ever something you need from me, please call. Honestly, a year down the road or ten, I'd welcome a phone call or a visit. You're quite a special young woman, and I've loved seeing you grow and shine over the last few months." She paused. Winked and squeezed Dre's hand. "Love becomes you."

Tears escaped then, and Dre moved to hug the woman who'd become so much more than a school professor to her. "Thank you. For everything."

***

Tom swung a leg over the horse and slid to the ground. Twenty head, most of them cow-calf pairs, spread out into the small gully before him at a wandering pace. Paul would be about done moving his group too, and they'd meet at the farmhouse. Sundown was still an hour away, but there wouldn't be enough time to move another group. He'd help restock the feed, make sure the firewood pile was full, and turn out the horses.

Then he'd head home for supper. Grams Rustin hadn't been doing well, and he didn't want her to feel like she needed to feed him. Besides, he wanted to call Dre. Was dying to know how her reveal went that morning.

The rustling of spring grass swished behind him. The work of the warm breeze at his back. He inhaled, taking in the smell of moist earth, the new life of spring, and the clean breeze that stirred around him.

"Taking a break?"

That voice. Hers. He knew it so well, often his thoughts would switch to her voice, if he was thinking something she'd say. Like, *For the love, Tom. Why do I miss you so much?* Or *You done just made me mad. Call me back when I can think straight.*

Hand on the saddle, Tom turned, expecting to see nothing but prairie, because Dre wasn't supposed to be home until the weekend. He was flying down to help her pack up her dorm room on Friday, after which, hopefully, they would know what came next.

The prairie was definitely not empty. The breeze toyed with her blond hair, making it dance against the clear blue sky, and she smiled as her jean-clad legs brought her closer.

"Dre?"

"Hey, cowboy." Her strides were bold, even as she picked around the scattered cactus and longer grasses between them. She didn't stop until her palm met his chest. "I missed you."

Still stunned, Tom barely breathed when she pushed upward for a kiss. His heart kicked hard, and as if jolted into a reality that seemed too good to be true, it took a breath or two before he kissed her back. But he did. Pulled her tight against him and tasted the heaven he'd been missing for weeks.

"What are you doing here?"

"Told you." She grinned. "You done took my heart, and I missed you too much."

He chuckled. "For the love."

"Exactly."

"What about your project?"

"Nailed it."

"But…"

"I caught the first flight I could book, and guess what? There's a little puddle jumper that makes that four-hour drive from Denver only a forty-five-minute flight to a little airport an hour south of here. So, surprise!"

"You hate flying."

"Worth it."

Her smile. He could keep that smile forever and never want anything more.

Tom's head swam. A little from that kiss, and it was tempting to dive back in and forget all the other questions that skittered in his mind. But also, because she was there. Right there in his arms when she was supposed to be in another state.

"I decided," Dre said.

"Decided?"

"This is home. With you, in Rock Creek."

"Dre..."

"Tom." She arched an eyebrow.

"Mrs. Cooper offered you a job. You should take it. It's what you've wanted. Worked for."

She nodded, the sass in her eyes fading. "It was. And I loved the project she let me do. But over the past weeks, I've slowly opened my grip on those dreams and plans. It's been freeing."

"Freeing?"

"Like, for some reason I thought I had to prove myself. Maybe because of those holes that we've talked about. But I stopped trying to cover them up, and you were right. Light gets in better when I don't get in the way."

"That doesn't mean you have to give up your dreams."

"I know. But they're different now. I see us here. Near our families. I see you, out here on this prairie you love so much. I see a new relationship with my brother, and I don't want to miss it. I see me spending the summers gardening with Mama, and canning with her in the fall." Her grin widened. "And I see me making sure you eat real vegetables with your meat and potatoes."

Tom laughed. "That right?"

She swayed in his arms, the sass in her coming out again. "That's right."

He lifted his hands from her hips to frame her cheeks. "Are you sure, Dre? Really, really sure?"

Her gaze on him didn't waver. "I am. I don't have to chase the world, or its expectations. There's beauty and possibilities right here, in this quiet, amazing life. The one I want forever with you."

Leaning in, he pressed his forehead against hers. "I like the sound of forever."

Her mouth briefly met his again. "Good. Then there's that ring shopping thing that we talked about..."

He laughed. "Right."

She turned, stepped under one of his arms, and after he gathered his horse's reins, they began walking back the way she'd come.

"I have a barn to visit too," Dre said. "Someone is going to have to make sure that beautiful old thing is used proper-like as it deserves."

"I know just the girl."

Epilogue

Twinkle lights drifted in beautiful wisps from the
rafters above.

The tables and hay bales covered with strips of white linen
sat to the side of the dance floor and out in the open grass of
the park. LED lanterns flickered in the dim light of the warm
summer evening as music drifted from inside the barn.

She'd started something all right. Dre grinned as she
scanned the scene.

"It's something." Tom's deep whisper tickled against her
neck as he slipped behind her and wrapped his suit-clad arms
around her body. "You know you still amaze me, right?"

She leaned back, not worried one bit about the fancy updo
that had taken nearly an hour to perfect earlier that day as she
snuggled into the man behind her. "Why on earth would you
say that?"

His low chuckle preceded a warm brush of his lips on her
neck. "Don't even pretend you didn't have this whole thing
dreamed up long before it was set in motion. I know you too
well."

Smiling, she turned in Tom's arms and welcomed the lips
that feathered her mouth. "That right?"

She felt his grin, and as he stepped back, she was able to fully
appreciate the man holding her. Blond waves of cropped hair,
defined jaw, warm steel-blue gaze that had, in fact, made her

rethink Texas. And hallelujah for that, because otherwise she'd have missed all this.

Coming home had been the best choice for her.

Deep satisfaction swelled within as she turned her contemplation over the people gathered within the barn. So many loved faces. Three kids who kind of made her world happier than she'd dreamed possible—two girls whose quiet personalities resonated with their dad's, and a boy who looked an awful lot like a young Tommy Kent but acted like a wild man. She said that was his uncle Paul in him. Her brother, a man who lived with both deep conviction and compassion, beginning his own new chapter with a woman Dre had come to love with all her heart. And her mama, holding on to joy even though the past year had rocked her world with sorrow.

Fourteen years of memories collected right there in that barn, not one of them she would trade for the most successful design business in all of Texas—or anywhere else for that matter.

We can't have it all, but we can sure love what we have. Or maybe, better put, who we have.

It'd been a long time, but Dre had recently reconnected with Tami Cooper. Mostly to say thank you. The budding renewal of friendship there came as an unexpected perk, and maybe some new possibilities Dre would have never expected.

"Look at that." Tom moved to the rhythm of the music, pulling Dre into a dance. "Have you ever seen Paul so happy?"

"Not that I remember." Dre leaned into Tom's shoulder, her attention still on her brother. And Suzanna, his bride. Heart bursting with joy, a few tears slipped over Dre's eyelids. This life. The ups and downs, the heartaches and hard choices, loved ones they'd lost, the fights and the make-ups, and the will to hang on...in all of it there was an ever-present impression of beauty. A whisper of unending Love that could inspire, guide, and redeem all things.

Light shining in holes she'd long since given up blocking.

Tom's hold on her tightened, and she snuggled into her husband.

"You never stop seeing it, do you?" he said.

"What's that?"

"Possibilities. Beautiful potential. In places most of us don't think to look. And here we are. In a barn that was never used for anything more than a storage unit until you showed us how awesome it could be, celebrating a wedding that wouldn't have happened if you hadn't challenged your brother to be nice to a woman he'd scornfully called *Pickle*."

Dre chuckled. Oh, Paul and Suzanna, what a start they'd had. And what a joy to see them on this side of it. She couldn't wait to see their life unfold together.

"I think you're giving me too much credit. I was just being a neighbor. And Suzanna's become a close friend. I'm glad to call her my sister."

Tom moved to tilt Dre's chin, bringing her gaze back to him. "I'm proud of you, and I get to say that because you married me, so don't argue."

"Oh." Dre laughed. "Okay. Anything else?"

"Yeah." He leaned down, mouth grazing hers. "I love you."

"Forever?"

His smile hovered deliciously over hers, reminding her of the day he'd proposed. The real one he'd given her after they'd gone ring shopping in Texas. He'd taken her back to the river for one last sit on her stone bench after they'd packed up her dorm. The hard goodbye had turned into a beautiful hello as Tom slid that shining new diamond on her finger.

Definitely a favorite memory.

"Forever," Tom promised yet again.

Arms wound around each other, they danced while their kids laughed and played among the crowd and her brother swayed with his new bride.

She was home. Still. And loved it with all her heart.

The End

Was this your first visit to Rock Creek? I really hope it's not your last! You'll find Paul and Suzanna's story in Reclaimed, which is a full-length novel (and actually, the first one I wrote of the Rock Creek Romances). You're also invited to meet some other residents of this charming little fictional town. Ordinary Snowflakes is about a single mom who is given a fresh chance at romance. In the romantic comedy The Cupcake Dilemma, you'll meet a quirky teacher who is a total kitchen disaster.

I hope you'll spend some time getting to know all these characters, and exploring more of Rock Creek.

Thanks for hanging out with Tom and Dre! I hope you enjoyed their story.

Rock Creek Romance Collection

Reclaimed

Just as Paul's kindness begins to melt Suzanna's frozen heart, a conflict regarding her land escalates in town. Even in the warmth of Paul's love, resentment keeps a cold grip on her fragile heart.

When romance isn't enough, will Suzanna ever find peace?

The Cupcake Dilemma

"Witty and sweet...an irresistibly fun and flirty read." -Rel, Relzreviewz.com

It all started with an extra assignment delegated to me at school right before Valentine's Day... But before we get too far, let me begin by stating this clearly. I was *voluntold*.

Ordinary Snowflakes

"…I have to pick myself up from the warm gooey puddle I've melted into on the floor. This book is perfection in a novella…" **-Katie Donovan, the Fiction Aficionado**

Someone has noticed me. A secret admirer? A man with a good heart, who sees how much I actually need help, even though I never admit it? Maybe this is the beginning of a beautiful story—a romance full of hope and second chances and love.

About the Author

JENNIFER RODEWALD IS PASSIONATE ABOUT THE WORD OF GOD AND THE POWERFUL VEHICLE OF STORY. THE DRAW TO FICTION HAS TUGGED HARD ON HER HEART SINCE CHILDHOOD, AND WHEN SHE BEGAN PURSUING WRITING, SHE SET ON STORIES THAT REVEAL THE GRACE OF GOD.

JEN LIVES AND WRITES IN A LOVELY SPECK OF A TOWN WHERE SHE WATCHES WITH AMAZEMENT WHILE HER CHILDREN GROW UP WAY TOO FAST, GARDENS, AND MARVELS AT GOD'S MIGHTY HAND IN EVERYDAY LIFE. FOUR KIDS AND HER OWN PERSONAL SUPERMAN MAKE HER HOME IN SOUTHWESTERN NEBRASKA DELIGHTFULLY CHAOTIC.

SHE WOULD LOVE TO HEAR FROM YOU! PLEASE VISIT HER AT **AUTHORJENRODEWALD.COM**.